THROUGH THE WITCHING GLASS

A Glass Slipper Adventure Book 7

Allie Burton

Allie Burton

Through the Witching Glass

A Glass Slipper Adventure Book 7

Copyright © 2023 by Alice Fairbanks-Burton

All rights reserved

INTRODUCTION

CONTENTS

PROLOGUE

My sister's grin sliced through any compassion I'd had for her.

A grin saying she'd won.

A grin dispatching me to purgatory.

My body plunged downward, through the sand and rocks and earth. Then, darkness with strange flashes of light in the distance. It was similar to traveling by portal through a witching glass or Alice falling down a rabbit hole. But I knew I wouldn't end up in some fantasy land.

I was going to the Underworld. To *helvete* or hades.

Except I wasn't dead. Yet.

The orange ball bound me in a blanket of fire as I fell. But I couldn't feel the scorching anymore. Maybe because I was enroute toward blazing Hades. Terror jolted and buzzed as if I were being connected to a hot wire. And I meant hot.

My lungs screeched but I didn't make a sound. Or maybe I did make a noise and no one could hear. Story of my life.

My speed slowed and I jerked before floating more than falling. I took a shaky breath. At least I wouldn't splat on the ground.

What about Mistress Lita? Was she flaming and falling like a crashing meteor?

The orange burned brighter and sizzled. My body suspended between life and death, light and dark. Fear and dread twitched in my veins. I twisted to see where I was aimed and squeezed my eyes shut. I didn't really want to know. The motion indicated I was going *down, down, down*.

The orange bubble confining me, and protecting me from falling faster, wavered into a cobalt blue. Broiling, blazing blue. My gaze flickered and prickled. I couldn't see anything except the bright light around me.

Was I dying?

I was gone and my sister Jinx was alive at the coven. My insides hardened. Surely, she'd tell someone about how I'd saved her and was missing. My friends saw the interaction. They would figure it out and find me. Doubt skewered. Jinx could continue to pretend to be me.

The bright blue morphed into yellow and orange and red. Thrashing in the constraints, I yelled. My ribs constricted and I blew out a long, slow breath. I had to stay calm.

Mistress Lita dropped past me. Her black gown flowed behind her. But she wasn't flying or floating. She dropped like a rock. Her expression stamped with anger and defeat. She didn't appreciate losing to my friend, Destiny.

Destiny had saved the coven and the kingdom. While I'd saved my undeserving sister. I'd never fall for Jinx's tricks again.

Wherever Mistress Lita and I were going, she'd arrive first. Maybe she could save us both. I had to cling to the hope that this wasn't my end.

The ball of fire flickered. The burning wasn't as intense. My floating slowed even more. My gut tightened. I was getting closer, but closer to what? I had no idea how the Underworld would feel, look, smell.

I drifted lower and lower. The colored bubble around me popped and disappeared.

And I fell. "Ahhhh!"

My body tensed and I hit hard ground. I waited for extreme pain, for death. Nothing happened. I checked my body with my hands. A few scrapes and bruises. Nothing life threatening. Was that a good thing?

Everything was dark, making it difficult to see in the distance. The ground I sat on was hard and warm. The air cloyed and suffocated.

A guttural growling caught my attention.

I crouched low and plastered myself against the wall of hot rock. I didn't know where I was. It was a cavern, similar to the one I'd been hiding in above. And yet this was different. A dark pall hung over the area and the stink of sulfur scalded my nose. I choked down a cry.

The growling came again, but this time the noise came from three different directions.

Ragged panic streaked through me.

"Hello? Destiny?" I swallowed, trying to hold down the hysteria rushing out. If my friend could hear me, she'd save me. "It's Cassia."

But my friend wouldn't be growling. She'd be cursing the mistress. And she hadn't been the one in the middle of the glowing ball spell. The magical ball that sent me down here.

Where exactly was here?

It was hot. Steaming hot. And dark. Too dark to see very far. A river roared nearby. But was it the upper Helvete River or the much lower River Styx?

All the oxygen evacuated my lungs, whooshing out of my mouth and becoming a surprised and fearful squeak. My pulse spiked. It couldn't be. Where else was possible? "I'm trapped on the banks of the River Styx."

Part of the Underworld and the gateway to hell.

My body quaked and heated. The overheating was expected. Look at my current location.

I tried to stay calm.

Mistress Lita had deserved to descend to purgatory. My sister, even though she'd been bad, didn't deserve to die. My heart cracked knowing she probably wouldn't have done the same for me.

"Jinx? Are you here?" I called out in a quivering voice to my sister just in case. Had I pushed her far enough away so she hadn't been affected? If so, she'd better try to find me.

With my gaze, I searched for an escape. Black rocks above and below. From what I recalled from books, the only exit was down the River Styx and I wasn't ready to die.

What would Destiny do? She'd said she'd spoken with the Dark Angel. Had she been on the banks?

"Destiny…" My tone weakened before it hit me that the mistress had fallen with me. "Mistress Lita!"

If I pretended to be Jinx, she'd help me.

My mind scrambled for ideas. Anything to give me hope.

I snapped my fingers to do a simple twinning spell to resemble my sister. This spell would only work for minutes unlike the spell Jinx had used. She'd had to bake a potion into a piece of cake for longevity. I snapped my fingers again.

Nothing happened.

Of course. Witch magic doesn't work on the banks of the River Styx. I'd read that in a book too. Only magic from the Dark Angel. Dark magic. Magic I didn't possess.

The thought thudded in my head. I had no powers to protect myself.

The growling grew louder, closer, and still came from three different directions.

I curled my legs up and pressed myself against the wall. My body trembled. How many terrifying animals were down here? My brain jolted. My near-perfect memory came up with the answer.

A cerberus.

According to history books, the three-headed dog helped guard the Gates to the Underworld. Known to be robust and fierce, the dog was trained in combat. One head represented the past, one the present, and the third the future.

Just then, the animal plodded into the open. Three heads. One body.

I was more terrified of the heads.

Three fang-filled mouths with slobber dripping. When the slobber hit the ground, it steamed. Three noses with wide, flaring nostrils. Surely, it could smell me. Six glowing eyes.

Horror curled inside and my muscles tensed. I'd be charred by the cerberus' flames or ripped apart before Destiny or Mistress Lita saved me. If Mistress Lita *would* save me. I wasn't sure considering she and Jinx had cooked up the scheme to kidnap and replace me.

My nerves wired tight. I patted the ground and picked up a thick stick, needing something to defend myself.

The white stick felt light and hollow. A bone.

I dropped it. "Ick!"

The monster dog huffed and pounced closer.

I grabbed the bone again. "Ew." Had it belonged to one of the kidnapped witches? One who was now dead? My mind filled in the scenario and I shuddered.

The dog stretched his heads and sniffed. He bent low, flexing his big, back paws with sharp nails. His rotund, muscular body went into a crouched position. He was about to spring an attack.

I scrambled back further against the wall, my lungs heaving. I couldn't catch enough oxygen. "Stay away." I held out the bone like a sword.

The dog angled his head, or should I say heads, watching me and the bone. More slobber came out of his mouths and he huffed. He'd tear me apart with his pointed teeth.

"Mistress Lita!" Desperation invaded and haunted my soul. I'd heard tales of the Dark Angel kidnapping young witches. A witch had been taken right in front of Destiny. "Destiny!"

The dog must've gotten tired of watching. He leapt toward me and thoughts of my friend vanished.

I pushed against the wall, tearing my sister's jeans. The dog growled and slobber dripped from his mouths onto my cheek. I clutched the bone, my singular defense. If it came near me, I'd swing.

Suddenly, a teenage boy loomed above me, flying. Dark wings spread out and his dark, wavy hair flopped in front of his face. Thick, dark eyebrows emphasized his bronzed skin and black eyes stared at me from above a straight-edged nose. His sculpted cheekbones and square jaw gave him an angular, yet manly appearance.

Before death I thought you were supposed to see your life flash before you, not a handsome hallucination.

He descended closer to me. His expression intensified and a gleam shown in his eyes. His mouth moved closer, pursing into a shape.

I took a shallow breath. Was he going to hurt me? Suck the air out of my lungs? I was more afraid of him than the cerberus. My body pressed against the wall. I couldn't get any closer. I couldn't move.

His mouth lowered, closer and closer.

My heart pounded in my chest, unable to escape the cage of my ribs.

He touched his lips to mine, caressing and...and kissing. He kissed me.

An electric zing went through my body and zapped my nerve endings. Shocked, my breath whooshed out and I pushed him away. I could still breathe. "What do you think you're doing?"

"Saving you." His thick lips twitched.

Wooziness filled my brain. Not from his kiss, or at least that's what I told myself. "You don't just kiss someone without asking."

"I kissed you to save you." He crossed his arms and his wings closed behind him.

I snorted. "You don't save someone from a cerberus with a kiss."

"Cerb just wants to play." The guy took the bone from my limp fingers and threw it.

The dog ran after the bone.

My body sagged. The cerberus behaved like a regular dog. I should've thought to throw the bone instead of hanging on to it. One threat gone.

The guy wore leather pants, a vest, and a black T-shirt. He resembled a biker, except he didn't need a motorcycle because he could fly. He held out his hand to help me. Or hurt me. I didn't know his plans.

I shifted away and my pulse continued pounding as it remembered his lips on mine. My first kiss and from a perfect stranger. But I only wanted a kiss from a certain werewolf. "Don't kiss me again."

"The kiss allows you to breathe in this atmosphere. My mom was able to stay on the banks of the River Styx with the Dark Angel because of the kiss."

My brow furrowed. "Your mom was the Dark Angel's Death Mate?"

"No." Sourness filled the single word. "The Dark Angel, my father, had already committed to someone. My mom was a witch he'd kidnapped. She died when I was twelve."

My immediate sympathy notched with confusion. "So your dad kissed your mom so she could breathe here? And now you have the same power and believed I needed your kiss?"

"Yes. You're a witch like my mom. The Dark Angel gave my mom the Kiss of Afterlife." A muscle in the cheek ticked. "Unlike Mistress Lita, my mom wanted to stay with him and me."

"I'm not staying." Determination rammed through me. "My sister will tell everyone what happened and my friends, Destiny and Stone, will rescue me."

And Lukas. Where was Lukas?

"There's no way out." The guy smiled again displaying devastating dimples and a crooked nose that looked as if it had been broken. "Mistress Lita finally died. My father and her traveled down the River Styx and through the Gates to the Underworld. I'm the new Dark Angel. The Archeron Barrier between worlds has closed. You're stuck here forever, Cassia."

Chapter One

Before the fall into the Underworld

I squeezed my sister Jinx's hand as we strolled toward our house in the Inferis Coven. She had run to greet me and wrapped me in a tight hug. She'd missed me. This time things would be different.

Excitement trilled, a hundred harps playing on my bones. After months in the dungeon under the human palace, and weeks in the banshee clan's captivity, I was finally free. Finally home.

And appreciated.

The sky wasn't sunny but today looked promising. My big sister held my hand in a tight grip as if she'd never let me leave again. At last, she paid attention to me, something she hadn't done since we were kids.

Which meant my parents would care too. Nerves jittered and I rubbed the beads hanging from the banshee bikini top I wore under my cloak. They had to care.

"Where are Mom and Dad?" *Why hadn't they come to greet me?*

"They're at home." Jinx tugged my arm, hurrying my steps. Her tall black boots and form-fitting orange dress didn't slow her down. "I heard a rumor at the academy that you'd returned and ran to find you."

"You could've sent Mom and Dad a smoke message." The messages took seconds to send and arrived immediately. With Jinx's powerful magic, she probably didn't even have to think about how to do the spell.

A green stream of envy, similar to her long glorious hair, sludged through my veins. *No.* I wasn't jealous of my powerful and beautiful sister anymore. I'd learned so much while I'd been away. Learned to use my sharp mind and proficient magic. Learned to be confident. I would no longer be overshadowed by my older sister.

"I was so excited you finally decided to come home." She sounded as though I'd stayed away on purpose. "I didn't even think to tell Mom and Dad."

Jinx always thought of herself first. Even as children, when we'd been best friends, she always led the games we played, decided when to snack, told Mom when our magic went awry. Usually blaming me. I frowned before shaking off the negative emotions. Jinx wasn't like that anymore. She'd been so nice in the messages we'd exchanged in between my dungeon imprisonment and my capture by the banshees, always asking about me. What I was doing, who I was with, where we were headed.

When our Victorian house came into view, I sucked in a deep breath trying to calm my anxiety and excitement. The front porch appeared welcoming. The curtains were closed in the recessed bay window so I couldn't see the interior. I'd be inside soon enough. The moonburst panels signaled our family's heritage and the geometric stained glass told stories about my ancestors. My gaze traveled up to the red pyramid-shaped turret piercing the gloomy sky. My bedroom was at the very top, not because it was the best room but because I had to climb dozens of stairs to get there.

"Our house looks the same." The thought reassured me.

"It is the same. Everything is the same." She emphasized the point for some reason.

I stood taller. I'd changed a lot. I'd never go back to being the meek little sister going along with my family's plans. "I'm not the same."

"Well of course not." She stopped, faced me, and stroked my hair—its hue more black than green. "You're more beautiful. If you'd just comb your hair and wear a little makeup to cover, you know, your tiny flaws. And that monstrosity on your forehead will have to go."

Relaxing, I soaked in her complimentary brew until the poison in her words hit me. It wasn't a compliment at all. Maybe she hadn't changed. And while I hated the tattoo the banshees had forcefully given me, it was a mark proving I'd survived. The powerful witch doctor of the coven could easily remove the tattoo eventually. But right now, I wanted to keep it as a reminder of my personal growth.

"And what's going on with you and the werewolf?" Jinx arched a black brow and puckered her lips.

My cheeks heated. She'd already figured out my unadmitted feelings for Lukas. Anxiety swirled in my stomach. Did Lukas realize I had a crush on him?

"The werewolf's name is Lukas. And nothing is going on between us. Yet." I didn't hold back my grin.

Her lips twisted in a calculating smile. "My baby sister has grown up."

"I'm taller than you so stop calling me a baby." The word inferred I was lesser somehow.

Not responding, Jinx flung open the front door. "Mom! Dad! Cassia is here!"

Taking another deep breath, I stepped across the threshold.

The scent of death attacked my senses, burning my nostrils. The cast iron stove wasn't lit so I wasn't sure what caused the stink. Then again, dirty dishes littered the coffee table along with a deck of cards featuring the custodians of death. Had my family become more wiccan or more sloppy? Of course, they hadn't had me here to clean.

The old-fashioned, tufted yellow sofa and matching chairs also had stuff lying on them. Discarded magazines, coats, an umbrella. It was hard to see everything with the curtains closed and the dim lighting from the wall sconces. The only natural light came from a stained glass window on the upper landing, the light showcasing a new pentagram etched into the wall and a skull sitting below on a small altar.

Maybe they had become more religious.

Spiral stairs led to the landing. And beneath the stairs was the mudroom and back door. I was already inclined to exit.

My parents didn't call out or come running. My body wilted. I'd never asked for much. I went along with my family's plans. I'd even taken the blame for Jinx's indiscretion so her position at the coven wouldn't be tainted. I hadn't expected to be dragged to the human dungeon for her mistake.

All in the past. I straightened my shoulders and ignored the smell, stepping further into the living room. A new chapter in my life was beginning.

"We are in the basement," Mom called from the stairway leading down.

My brow scrunched. "Why are they down there?"

The door leading downstairs was open. The basement used to hold the potions cellar, but my parents let it go to ruin by shoving misused or broken items behind the barred door. They didn't fill the stocks of ingredients. Rats scurried across the floor. Musty and smelling of cat urine, whenever anyone needed something, they'd forced me to search down there. I shuddered.

"We have a surprise for you." Jinx squeaked, unable to contain her excitement.

She was excited for me which was unusual.

I beamed, brightening my insides. Maybe they'd bought me a present too big to wrap. Or maybe they'd cleaned the cellar for me to use now that I was back and would be attending Inferis Academy again. Potions were my specialty and I'd hated when they'd neglected the potion storage room. Or maybe my familiar had arrived. I was sixteen and every other witch my age already had a familiar. Jinx's slimy snake had shown up when she'd turned thirteen.

Anticipation slid up my spine as I went down the stairs. I reached the bottom step, waiting for them to flicker the light on and yell surprise. "Mom? Dad?"

Thick arms wrapped around me and the cloak I wore became a straitjacket. I inhaled the bergamot scent of my father's cologne. "Da—"

His arms squeezed tighter and he lifted me off the ground. Air rushed out of my lungs. What was happening? This was no hug. My arms stuck to my sides and I couldn't lift my hands.

"Shut up." He carried me with my feet dangling.

"Dad?" My body slumped for a second in shock before twisting, trying to get away. From my big giant of a father. I continued to fight, kicking with my hard sandals.

Confused thoughts ran circles in my brain. This wasn't a good surprise. Horror scraped, hollowing my chest. I'd been confined too many times over the last several months. I refused to let him trap me. I kicked harder.

"Oof." His muffled oath gave me a bit of satisfaction.

"Hurry, dear. Before she uses magic against us." My mom's voice trembled. She was in on this.

Whatever this was.

It made no sense. Why would I use magic against my own parents? Sure, they'd given me up to the human guards for something Jinx had done, but I thought they'd welcome my return, be proud of me and what I'd accomplished. Fighting against the evil regent. Helping my friend Destiny escape the banshees. Assisting the new king, King Zacharye. I told Jinx everything in my letters.

I struggled more. "Jinx? What's going on?" At least she'd been nice and welcoming.

Metal creaked.

"The cellar door is open." Jinx's glee vibrated in her tone. She was in on it too. This was all fun and games to her.

Not to me. Hurt spiraled through my heart as if a drill were going through the center. My sister was part of this betrayal.

"Put me down." Struggling against my dad's arms, I tried to see through the blackness. Confusion was a darkness of its own. This wasn't the welcome I'd expected.

"Will do." Dad dropped me, released his arms, and shoved with his thick hands.

I stumbled forward while my emotions tumbled from disbelief and confusion to resentment and anger. I put my hands out. "What the broomstick?"

Falling physically, mentally, and emotionally, I'd been a fool. I hit the cold, damp concrete floor of the basement and twisted around to scramble to my feet. I wiped my sweaty hands on my skirt.

The bars of the cellar door clanged shut.

The noise echoed in my mind and reverberated through my body. My mouth dropped open. I didn't know what to say. I ran toward the metal bars and gripped them, rattling them with my anger. "Let me out."

A tiny tip of light brightened and moved around in the darkness.

My gaze followed the light with frantic motion. "Is that your wand? Are you using a spell against me?"

"I'm spelling the lock so you can't mess with it." Jinx snapped her fingers and the overhead lightbulb flickered on.

I blinked a couple of times and slowly pivoted.

The small potions cellar appeared worse than before I'd left. Not only was the potions cabinet practically empty, but the entire piece of wooden furniture had fallen. Bits of wood, old droppers, and bottles littered the ground. The books that had been stored neatly on a shelf were now haphazardly stacked on the floor with spines broken and pages torn out. A couple of crates sat in the corner.

"Why are you locking me in the old potion cellar?"

The left side of Jinx's lips lifted in a twisted smirk. Her narrowed gaze flashed with superiority. Bitterness tasted on my tongue. I should've known the loving sister routine was an act.

Raising my hands, I had to use my own magic to stop whatever spell she put on the lock. I'd learned things while I was away.

"Magic doesn't work on that side of the cellar." My dad's bushy mustache twitched with a slight smile proving they'd thought this scheme through. His large body heaved with the exertion from carrying me. He'd gotten larger since I'd last seen him. "Behind the bars."

I remembered. Ingredients used to be stored and mixed in the cellar. Occasionally, if magic was needed for a potion, you'd have to step through the bars to the other side of the basement. A large worktable sat nearby, just on the other side.

"Look at her forehead." Mom screeched, her height a foot lower than my father's. Her wide gray eyes flashed with disgust and her painted lips dropped open. "She resembles a banshee."

Glancing at the low, moldy ceiling, I shivered. I'd been excited to return to my family and coven. I'd wanted to prove to everyone how much I'd changed, how I'd helped my friends escape from the palace dungeon and a wicked banshee clan too. I'd wanted to introduce my friends. I understood I wasn't the main attraction of the group—that would be Destiny with her unusual powers—but I'd been part of the team and she was my best friend. I hadn't expected to be locked up upon return.

"Another sign that Cassia has been corrupted." Dad tucked his chin into the rolls of fat around his neck.

"Hanging out with banshees, werewolves, giants, fairies, and trolls. They've poisoned your magical purity." Mom patted her black and gray hair hanging past her shoulder. Wrinkles I'd never noticed before etched around her mouth and eyes. "It's for your own good, Cassia."

My brows shot up. My mother was horrified by my friends. Prejudiced. "They're my friends. Why don't you want me to be with them?"

"We're your family. Not them." Dad's terseness held in his anger.

I took a step back. They didn't act like family, hadn't in years. I should've realized it when my parents told the human guards I'd used magic to change a cheating human boyfriend into a toad—Jinx could've been more original. My parents had known she'd committed the crime.

Now, I was paying again. "Why are you doing this to me?"

My parents exchanged a glance.

"You can't be seen like that." Mom shook her head and revulsion showed on her face.

"And those clothes." Dad's gaze raked my body and I wrapped the cloak tighter around the bikini top and short skirt. "You're not decent."

"I can change my outfit. I can go upstairs right now." All the clothes in my closet were less revealing than the banshee outfit. All my clothes were less revealing than the outfits Jinx wore every day.

"The bars holding Cassia are reinforced with Mistress Lita's special magic." Satisfaction oozed in Jinx's voice as she explained the details to my parents. She puffed out her chest, straightened her shoulders, and beamed. She was proud she'd used the coven leader's magic.

I reeled back. Did Mistress Lita approve of my family holding me prisoner? This wasn't about the banshee mark on my forehead or the clothes I wore. This captivity had been planned. Which meant my family or the coven leader wanted something. Not from me, but from my friends.

Apprehension heaved in my gut. My friends were in danger. And I couldn't warn them.

Because I'd been locked in another cage.

Chapter Two

My home had become my new prison.

The iron bars taunted me, separating me from freedom and my friends.

I sneezed from the dust. The constant dripping of water from pipes was torture. Covering my ears, I peered through the bars. Beside the worktable sat an old rocking chair and boxes filled with junk.

Fleeting thoughts bolted and zigzagged in my brain about the circumstances of my new captivity. For a second, I thought it must be a joke. A funny homecoming we'd laugh about later. Then, I'd believed it was because of how I appeared with the banshee mark on my forehead. But after spending an uncomfortable night on an old wingback chair, and no one had come to remove the tattoo, I'd known something sinister was at play.

The dripping stopped and a rushing of water came through the pipes. A toilet flushing.

"Oh gross." My family continued to live their normal lives while keeping me in the basement.

Outrage pounded and powered through me. My fingers tingled. But no magic came. I clenched my hands into fists. Home and yet not free.

The door to the basement creaked open and light footsteps came down the stairs.

"Who's there?"

"That's no way to greet your mother, Cassia." Mom came down the stairs wearing a simple housecoat and slippers. She was carrying a tray.

"Are you my mother?" I fisted and flexed my hands. "Or has some alien taken your place?"

Her face paled and a flash of fear entered her eyes. I knew she wasn't scared of me. "Of course I'm your mother. Don't be silly." Wheeling away, she set the tray down while avoiding my gaze.

"A real mother wouldn't lock their daughter in a cage." I grabbed a book and threw it toward the bars.

The book thumped and fell to the ground.

"It's only for a little while." Her gaze darted around. "Jinx is working on a special project and you'll get in the way."

My muscles tightened. Of course, Jinx wanted something. My parents locked me up for her. I wanted to explode with anger. "And what Jinx wants, she gets."

Bitterness swamped my mouth. This had always been the dynamics of the family. Jinx wanted a cat and we got one, even though I'd wanted a dog. Jinx received new clothes and I was given her hand me downs because she was the oldest. Jinx caused trouble and I got blamed.

I'd taken this unfairness in stride. She was older and more powerful. And she'd always been on my side. She'd told me if she wasn't allergic to dogs, I could've had one for a pet. She'd begged my parents to buy me new clothes because I was too large to fit in her old ones. She'd always explained how even if she'd done the damage, somehow it was truly my fault. And I'd always believed her.

Until now.

"Your sister works hard for Mistress Lita while finishing school. You should be proud of her." My mom clearly was proud of what Jinx had accomplished. I was not.

Jinx cheated, schemed, and lied to get what she wanted. The coven leader's connection to the scheme dug in my mind. "Are my friends in danger?"

"Not if they do..." Mom slapped her hand over her mouth.

My gut clenched. "Not if they do what?" I leaned forward anxiously waiting for her answer.

"Nothing." She slid the tray through a small slit at the bottom of the door. "Here's your breakfast."

Mushy oatmeal steamed in a bowl. No fruit. No milk or tea.

"Wow, you're *almost* treating me better than the banshees." My earlier bitterness returned and sarcasm spewed out of my mouth. "Or the guards in the palace dungeon."

Her gaze flared with remorse. At least I hoped it was remorse. "Don't give me a hard time. I had to argue to give you these comforts. Do you want breakfast or not?"

Annoyance spiked and I curled my lips. She obviously wasn't in charge of my captivity. I had to play on her love for me. If she had any. Jinx was better at manipulating our parents.

Sniffing, I swiped at my cheeks, pretending to hold in tears. "Thank you, Mom."

I stretched my arm through the bars, trying to touch her, and she jumped back. Was she afraid of me or what Dad or Jinx would do to her?

"I know how much you care about me, Mom. I missed you so much while I was gone." I acted like the lost little girl they assumed I was. "I'm just a little confused. What's happening in the coven? What project?"

She stiffened. "I can't speak of it."

"Why?"

Fearful, she twisted her hands together and glanced up the stairs. "Because if a certain someone found out I blabbed, I'd be sent to the Underworld."

Gripping hold of the bars, I tilted back. "The Underworld?"

Not answering, she stomped up the stairs leaving me to wonder.

I'd read about the Underworld and the Dark Angel. My brow furrowed, remembering other things I'd learned. This particular Dark Angel had a penchant for kidnapping young witches. I'd been warned at a young age to stay away from Dark Angel's Veil, a tumultuous waterfall close to the Archeron Barrier between the coven and the Underworld.

Is that what my mother was afraid of? Being thrown into the falls to descend into the Underworld and die? Or, since the Dark Angel kidnapped teen witches, would I be the one thrown into the falls if things don't go according to plan?

Did my family believe they were protecting me by locking me up?

⋙ ⋘

I paced the small space and kicked a dirty, plastic funnel. The funnel rolled across the floor, hitting the back wall and almost going through a small hole. So that's how the rats got inside the cellar. A problem for another day.

I'd created a palette to sleep on with the cushions from the chair and an old blanket. I'd organized the few potions left on the shelves, including Baneberry and Dandelion root. I'd read several old potion books, one of which had been buried beneath the shelves and was so ancient the pages crinkled and cracked.

Several days had passed and I was still locked in the potion cellar. I'd tried to pick the lock. I'd found an old metal file and tried to saw through the iron bars. I'd taken the wingback chair and rammed it against the bars, the walls, and the ceiling. My mom had yelled at me to quit making noise.

Frustration bubbled in a brewing potion. My head steamed. I had no idea what was happening in the coven or to my friends.

My friends must have realized I was missing. How was my family explaining my absence? Destiny must've inquired about me by now. She'd realize something was up and find me.

The door above the stairs opened and light footsteps treaded down. My shoulders dropped. Jinx. Each visit she either tried to get more information about my friends or teased me mercilessly.

"Cassia! Guess who I kissed today." She strutted down the wooden steps, fluffing her long, green hair and acting like a runway model. She smoothed the plain black dress she wore over her hips. My dress—one of my favorites.

"Why are you wearing my clothes?" I demanded.

She glanced down and scrunched her nose before scowling at me and twisting her lips into a malicious smile. "I kissed Lukas."

Her sing-songy tone scraped across my skin and my heart stopped beating for a second. Anguish cascaded through my chest. The first guy I'd ever liked and he was so easily persuaded by my sister's charms.

"Good for you." Holding in a sniff, I couldn't display his importance to me. I'd already admitted I had a crush on him and she'd gone after him anyway. Or was she lying? I didn't know what to believe anymore. I was living in an upside-down world.

She brought out a plate she'd hidden behind her back.

The sweet smell of devil's chocolate cake tickled my nose and I licked my lips. At this moment, I wanted cake more than Lukas. "Is the cake for me? Because you *supposedly* broke my heart?"

"This is for me." Jinx held out the plate in front of me, tempting me. "I've been eating a lot of cake lately."

Hunger and hurt jabbed and I couldn't help poking back. "Is that why you can't wear your own clothes? You can't fit in them any longer?"

"Finally, you admit you're fat." Her smile switched to secretive and sly. "You've grown bold, baby sister. But I wish I didn't have to wear your clothes."

"I'm not fat." I slammed my palms against the bars. My clothes were bigger because I didn't wear them so tight that every curve of my body showed. This cruel teasing had to stop. I had more important things to ask. "Why pull Lukas into whatever crazy scheme you have planned?"

"Curiosity, and for fun." She puckered her lips. "Does it annoy you that I kissed him after you? Do you think he'll compare us?"

"I've never kissed him." I crossed my arms as anger quivered. My statement—while I wished it wasn't true—might prove Lukas wasn't important to me, that if she'd picked him just to strike at me it wouldn't work.

"Of course, you haven't." She tapped a fork against the plate she carried. "I was shocked the human guards actually believed you we're the one who kissed the human and turned him into a toad."

"You did that!" Rushing the metal bars, I pounded against them.

"Well, we won't have to worry about human guards anymore. Mistress Lita has locked down the coven now that your special friend has arrived."

Special friend? Was she talking about Lukas?

I glared at the stupid cushions I'd slept on.

"Oh my stars!" I gripped the bars tighter. "You can't keep me here forever. Someone's going to figure out I'm missing and my friends will ask about me."

"I always forget that stupid saying of yours. *Oh my stars.* So positive. *Oh moons* suits me better. It's dark and cunning." She took a bite of the cake and emphasized the chewing motion. "Anyway, you told me you liked Lukas. I can't believe my sweet, boring sister wants a werewolf."

Each nosh ground against my own teeth. I wasn't sweet and boring. Sure, I might've preferred not to be the center of attention, but I wasn't invisible. I wrapped the thick banshee cloak around my body. Lukas had liked me until Jinx came along.

"Although the werewolf was quite tasty. What I do with the werewolf next," she winked, "will be *wild*."

My heart plunged, taking my confidence down with it. He'd so easily taken the bait without even considering me.

"Get it? *Wild*." Jinx's cruel chortle cut through my pain. She took another bite of cake.

I got it. Lukas was a werewolf. But he didn't deserve to be treated as a pet or a possession. My sister didn't care for him. She'd use him and toss him aside like she did all the guys in her life. He'd hate me forever because of my sister. "Leave Lukas alone."

She gave me an insincere, evil grin and took another bite. "I've done a little studying on werewolves."

"You studied?" I emphasized my astonishment. She never read books or did her assignments. She'd blackmailed me into helping her, explaining how her success would help my success. I'd believed her.

She glowered and stuck the last bite of cake into her mouth. "Werewolves bond to each other using a chemical signature. They mate for life."

My stomach flipped. Was she saying Lukas would love her forever? Even after she dumped him? Because *she would dump him*.

Hot, red explosions went off in my bloodstream. My knuckles turned white gripping the bars of my captivity. Lukas would be linked to my sinister sister for his entire life. While she felt only contempt for him.

Jinx slammed the glass plate on the worktable beside the bars. Taking out a small compact mirror with silver etchings of stars and moons, she stared at her reflection. "Mistress Lita gave me this mirror. It has powerful magic." Her smile hitched. "Outside those bars."

I gritted my teeth at her tease.

Her long green hair shortened and tinted to a black and green mix. Identical to mine. Her face became rounder and her eyes flickered into gray. My color. Her cheeks became fuller and a little pale.

I gawked and sucked in a long, slow breath watching the transformation. My pulse stopped and then raced forward. Jinx looked exactly like me.

"The cake is a special spelled recipe from the mistress." She smirked at me with *my mouth*. "Think about it. Your first kiss with the werewolf and it wasn't really you."

My first kiss with anyone. I'd never been interested in the pompous warlocks in the coven, and they had only been interested in my powerful sister.

So not what I should be thinking about right now.

Jinx appeared identical to me. It was like peering in the mirror, except she didn't sport the banshee tattoo on her forehead. My body froze, cooling to my core.

She fluffed *my* hair and scrunched *my* nose as if she didn't appreciate what she saw in the mirror—which was me.

I tried to fathom the meaning of her actions.

"Your zauber friends won't ask for you or search for you." She spewed the insulting slur as if it didn't refer to her too. Snapping the compact closed, she tossed it on the table next to the discarded plate. "Because you're not missing. And as an added bonus, you're now more cool and confident."

She stabbed me with a final insult and left the room.

Left me gaping in shock and awe. Left me wondering why she would want to pretend to be me. Left me pondering what trouble she planned to cause in my name.

Chapter Three

I needed to escape now more than ever.

Before I thought my family's scheme only impacted me. I was wrong. Over the past several days—so many that I couldn't keep count—I tried to break down the bars. I tried to convince my mom to let me out. I tried reaching through the bars and using magic. Nothing worked. I knew my friends wouldn't search for me because they didn't know I was missing. They'd be hurt by my sister's plot. This wasn't just about her kissing Lukas.

I rattled the bars causing the worktable to shake and the compact my sister had used to slide off onto the floor. Glass shattered. I didn't care about ruining my sister's mirror. If it had magic, it might be useful.

I laid on the ground and stretched my arm through the bars. My fingers inched toward the compact and grazed across the gold edge. The compact slid further away. I sunk further into the floor. I couldn't reach the mirror.

Giving up wasn't an option. If I ever got to a spot where magic was accessible, the compact could help.

Swinging my body around, I stuck my leg between the bars. I pushed my leg as far as it could go with my body smashed against the bars. Grasping out with my toes, I grazed the compact again. My leg throbbed. I had to get the mirror. I gripped the compact between my toes and nudged it closer and closer and closer. Pulling my leg out, I swished around, stuck my arm through, and grabbed the compact.

Accomplishment pumped in my veins, matching my pulse.

I flipped the compact open. The mirror was cracked. Would it have power? I couldn't test it in the potion cellar. Wrapping my fingers around the compact, I squeezed tighter letting my anger and frustration build.

My parents had gone along with Jinx's plan. My ribs constricted creating a tight, demoralized, hard-to-breathe sensation. I'd always known my sister and I weren't treated equally. But I never expected this level of complicity from my parents. I'd been anxious to return to the coven to show off the new me. To prove to them I'd survived the dungeon and captivity by the banshees, and I'd thrived. I could've become an important member of the community like my sister.

My friends wouldn't search for me unless they realized the duplicitous duplication. Jinx might resemble me, but she didn't act like me. Although they might put the changes down to me being home. They'd forget the real me. I had to get free to save Lukas from my sister's attentions and my friends from whatever plot Jinx and Mistress Lita had brewed up.

I surveyed the room again. Out of boredom, I'd salvaged and placed a few potions on the shelves at the back of the room. Most of the bottles were empty. I'd searched the potions after the first night in the cold, damp cellar and hadn't been able to find any concoction to break the bars.

The spell Jinx cast was strong.

Pacing the room, I had to figure out how to get free. I was smart. There had to be a way. Dropping to the floor, I laid on my back and slammed my feet into the bars, more out of frustration than anything. The bars stayed put.

A brown rat ran past my head, its tiny feet tangling in my hair.

I cringed, shoving the rodent away and jumped to my feet. "Ah!"

The rat scrambled across the concrete floor and escaped through the tiny hole in the wall by the funnel I'd thrown.

"If only I was that small." An idea flashed.

Small.

There was a potion in one of the books I'd read on how to make pets or familiars smaller. Would it work on me?

I dashed to the book lying on the floor. It had a dark spine, worn from age. A raised compass-like device locked the book, but due to the book's terrible treatment, the lock easily flipped open. I thumbed through the yellow, crinkly pages.

"Spellshield of Light, Morphectus, Incantation for Spirits." I stabbed my finger when I found the correct page. "Accipere Parvus. Get Small."

Triumph drummed. Being smart and remembering things wasn't sad as my sister always told me. She might have more powerful magic, but I had a more powerful brain.

I read through the list of ingredients. "Baneberry. That's on the shelf. Dandelion root. There's a bit at the bottom of a potion bottle. It might be enough." Anticipation brewed like this potion would be doing soon.

"I can use the dust off the shelves for dead skin cells." My finger stopped at the bottom of the list. "Alkali. I don't remember seeing alkali."

Quickly, I moved to the wall and skimmed the few potions left. I pulled out each small drawer and peered inside, mostly empty. When my grandmother was alive, we'd been one of the favorite suppliers to the mistress. But neither of my parents had an affinity for potions. I'd inherited the talent. Now, we must be doing other nefarious things for the leader.

I found drops of dried dragon blood and fire seed to maintain the high temperature. "No, alkali." I tapped my finger on my chin. My gaze scoured the small cellar and the room outside. Nothing.

The solid idea was just out of reach. My fingers tingled imagining creating the potion. A potion using only ingredients, not magic. A potion I could make on this side of the bars. I had to find a way.

Before one of my parents or Jinx visited again, I hid the stuff I'd gathered and the book. They couldn't know I had an escape plan or they'd find a way to crush it. I had to play it cool. Agony click-clacked in the slowest countdown clock. When the clip clop of high heeled boots finally came down the stairs, I knew this was my chance.

"Our plan is working perfectly." Jinx tugged on her hair—hair resembling mine. "Soon, I'll have your friend Destiny convinced of the right thing to do."

"And what would that be?" I still didn't know Jinx's scheme. "It must be the wrong thing if you want *my* friend to do it."

"You, me. At this point no one knows the difference." Jinx's cruel laughter ramped up my fear and anger.

I couldn't make her mad. I had to appear sad and pathetic. "Except I stink."

She sniffed. "You smell like eau de mold."

"Let me take a bath. Please." I put my hands together in a pretty please pose. "I can't take the stench any longer and soon it will be wafting up the stairs to your bedroom."

If it affected her, she'd be more likely to do something.

She scrunched her nose. "I already have to wear your ugly clothes. I'd hate to smell like you too." Her lips twisted together and she smirked. "Besides, Lukas is accustomed to my smell."

Her cruel tease didn't dampen my hope. If she let me out to take a shower, I could escape without using the more risky plan.

"You can wash up." She snapped her fingers and a bar of soap and a wet washcloth appeared in her hand.

My fingers quivered seeing magic working just on the other side.

A memory flashed and I thought about my friend Violet. Back in the dungeon, she'd realized her fairy magic worked just past the guards and she'd flown toward them, used her magic, and was shot in the process. The witch doctor was supposed to be taking care of her here at the coven. I didn't believe that anymore. A chill went through me. She was in as much danger as my other friends, completely at the coven's mercy.

My stomach clenched. I had to know. "What happened to my friend Violet? I sent her here for medical help."

"The frozen fairy?" Jinx chuckled.

Had she always made fun of others' issues? Did she believe other people, other majiks didn't matter? My memories were of a loving sister, although she always found ways to put me down. She'd only become cruel when she reached her final year at the academy and became popular.

"Yes, the fairy." The coven probably didn't house many other majiks. "Her name is Violet."

"She's being cared for by the witch doctor. Her condition hasn't changed." By her tone, Jinx didn't care.

"Speaking of conditions." I smelled the cloak I'd worn for days. "What about clothes for after I wash up?" If my more risky plan worked I didn't want to be running around in the low-hipped skirt and bikini top with beads dangling and making noise, giving my position away.

"You can continue wearing the banshee outfit while I have to suffer in this ugly dress." She picked at the long, star-patterned skirt molding to her hips. "Did you ever buy a dress or skirt cut above your knees?" No point in answering her rhetorical question. "If I have to wear your clothes, you have to wear what I say."

The dress had been in the back of my closet because it was too short and too tight. It appeared even tighter on Jinx. But she loved the ogles and attention.

"Your choice. Or you can stop this scheme right now and let me go." I held my breath hoping something would convince her, knowing it wouldn't.

"Have a nice sponge bath." Jinx pushed the soap and washcloth between the bars then trotted up the stairs, leaving me alone.

If she and the mistress succeeded in their evil scheme, what would happen to me? To Destiny and Lukas? To Violet and my other friends? I had to stop whatever they planned. I picked up the bar of soap. Determination firmed my spine. Jinx had unknowingly given me the final ingredient for the potion.

Instead of washing up, because I didn't want to waste the soap, I gathered the ingredients I'd hidden. I started measuring and mixing in an old cauldron from one of the bottom shelves. A pinch of dust, a dash of baneberry, everything left of the dandelion root, and a drop of dragon blood. I used an old mortar and pestle to smash the fire seed and added it to the mix. Now, I needed the alkali.

Picking up the soap, I'd read that a bar of soap had an alkali level somewhere between eight and ten. I knew I couldn't drop the bar in the cauldron. It wouldn't mix. I searched for something to carve the soap, rummaging through the junk on the shelves and the garbage on the floor. Of course, my family hadn't cleaned the cellar before locking me up, but they had removed any sharp objects.

I couldn't give up.

I flipped open the compact I'd swiped and studied the shards of glass. The circular piece had a crack creating a thin crescent. I could use the shard to cut the soap. Using the pointy end of the pestle, I pried the narrow piece out.

"Ouch." Blood dripped from my finger and I shook it. What was one wound when I was about to drink a potion I'd never made before? I could be poisoning myself. My body stiffened.

What was I doing? I could *poison* myself.

Shaking my head, I squeezed the piece of glass between my fingers. I was good at potions. It was my best subject at the academy. I could do this. I had no other choice. Slicing the soap, I let the narrow pieces drop into the cauldron. This was the Accipere Parvus or Get Small potion. Next, I had to make the antidote.

After pouring the potion into an empty bottle, I mixed the ingredients for the Crescere or Grow potion and put it in another bottle. A much smaller bottle and a less complicated spell even with my limited ingredient stock. I marked both.

Now, I just needed a guinea pig. Or a rat.

I pulled out one of the rat traps that hadn't worked and set a piece of cheese from my last meal. Holding a wood crate, I waited for the rat to spring my trap.

A rat with its cute little pink ears and twitching nose peeked out of the hole in the wall. He stood on his back legs and sniffed more. His beady black eyes spotted the cheese. He ran forward and I dropped the crate over him.

"Sorry, Mr. Rat." I filled a dropper with the Get Small potion and grabbed his furry body. Stroking his fur, I tried to comfort the little guy. "Hopefully this doesn't have a soap taste."

The rat sucked on the dropper.

Flipping over the crate, I set him back inside. "Too bad I don't have a measuring tape." I took the marker I'd used to label the potion bottles and drew a line in the crate at the rat's current height.

Crossing my fingers, I watched and waited. My gaze rounded with each passing second. The rat doubled over. His body twitched and lurched. He fell on the ground, wriggling. He appeared to be in pain.

Guilt speared through me making my midsection cramp. I didn't want to hurt the guy. And any pain he felt, I'd experience on a larger scale. What if I got so small my internal organs failed?

The rat stilled on the ground.

My lungs scraped with horror and my eyes stung. Had I killed the rat? Would I die too?

Leaning forward, I examined him. He was definitely smaller. The potion worked. But had I killed him in the process? "Mr. Rat?"

The rat's beady gaze flickered open. He scrambled to his feet. I wished he could talk to me or at least communicate like a witch's familiar or a dragon.

I grabbed the back of his neck. Setting him on his back paws, I held him by the line I'd drawn. He was smaller.

Success boomed. The rat had shrunk. The potion worked.

Would it work on a human? Could it make me small enough to fit through the hole in the wall? And what if the first potion worked and the second didn't?

I'd be small forever.

Uncertainty and anxiety braided together and I pushed it aside. I couldn't worry about what ifs. The rat was definitely smaller. "How are you feeling, Mr. Rat?"

Obviously, he didn't answer.

Time for the second test.

I filled the dropper with the Grow potion and gave it to the rat.

The rat's body went rigid in my hand. His fur felt cold. His mouth gaped open as if he couldn't breathe. Horror fluttered and scraped in my chest once again. Was the second potion killing him? He'd gone stiff as a board.

The rat's feet twitched. His body slimmed and elongated. He grew and grew and grew. He was now taller than the line on the crate, big enough to peek out the top.

"It worked!" I jumped up and down. "Both potions worked!"

Taking the piece of cheese off the trap, I set it by the hole in the wall. Then, I picked up the crate and set it on its side by the cheese. "Thank you, Mr. Rat."

He grabbed the cheese, crouched down, and scampered through the hole.

Realization killed my excitement. The real test was on me. Nerves ping-ponged around my brain and landed with a thud in my stomach. The rat hadn't died, although he'd experienced intense pain. He'd shrunk and grown. I didn't know if I'd caused any real damage. Frowning, I stared at the hole he'd run through. The same hole I planned to use for my escape.

My hands trembled as I picked up the Grow potion and slid it into the hole in the wall. Using the open compact, I pushed the small bottle even further inside. I used the mirror to try to see if the space on the other side was big enough for regular-sized me. It wasn't. I dropped the compact and left it there. I'd have to move the Grow potion bottle to a spot where I could grow.

Anxiety reeled, but this was the plan I'd come up with, the only feasible idea. I was an expert at potions. My first year at the academy, I'd advanced to the cutting-edge potions class. This had to work.

Rubbing my hands together, I stared at the Get Small potion.

I was tired of being kidnapped and locked away because of other people. First, Jinx had used magic for revenge and I'd been imprisoned in her place. Then the banshees kidnapped me because of Destiny. And now...now I didn't know what my sister and parents had planned. All I knew was that Jinx wanted everyone to believe she was me.

Time to rescue myself. Or die trying.

I picked up the bottle, took a deep breath, and drank the rest of the Get Small potion.

Chapter Four

The potion burned down my throat. The liquid scorched my lungs and flamed in my belly, scalding and blistering. I doubled over in torment. Sweat formed, dripping down my body in rivulets and pooling on the ground. My heart thumped. I was going to die.

My entire body seared and was hot to the touch. My skin furrowed and puckered. I felt mushy and squishy. Following the sweat, my skin hung from my frame. Ooh, I was melting.

The banshee outfit I wore drooped on my shrinking body. The shula skirt fell off my hips. The bikini top hung around my neck like a large necklace.

I. Was. Shrinking.

And naked.

If I wasn't in so much pain, I'd think about the time I stole the regent's clothes and he'd run out of the banshee tent nude. The joke was on me. If I survived, I'd be defenseless and naked. Normally, my cheeks would redden with embarrassment from having no clothes, but I was so overheated, I didn't care.

Of course, I was also alone.

The potion bottle slipped from my smaller fingers. It hit the concrete floor and shattered. Pieces of glass flew like projectiles.

Agony screeched through me. My bones hurt and my veins throbbed. My head wanted to explode. I panted, trying to calm my unstable body, trying to stay standing. Rounding my shoulders, I waited for what would come next.

My body compressed and deflated.

I became shorter and shorter and shorter and shorter. My pulse beat faster and faster and faster and faster. My eyes grew bigger as the world around me swelled and expanded.

No, the world wasn't changing. I was.

My lungs constricted and I let out a shriek. Cooling, I blinked a few times. I was small, but alive. The potion had worked.

My elation tamped down with fear. Being small could be dangerous.

Slapping a hand to my chest and torso and legs, I checked to make sure everything was in the right place. I was now three inches tall.

The spine of the thick potion book came to my shoulders. The crate towered above me. The potion cellar that had barely contained me now appeared palatial. I couldn't reach the velvet on the chair and the lowest shelf on the wall was way above my head. The tiny shards of glass scattered around had become as large as a standing mirror. I could see my entire body.

And I was still naked.

Climbing down from my huge sandals, I picked up the damp washcloth and wrapped it around my body, tucking the terrycloth beneath my arms.

I looked like me. The same black and green hair. The same wide gray eyes. The same upturned nose. The same banshee mark on my forehead. I gave myself a final glance. It was me, but different. Smaller but stronger. I was in control of my destiny and it was time to act.

Taking a step, I covered an inch of ground. At this rate, it would take me years to get to the front door of the house. Good thing I had the Crescere Get Big potion. Anxiety curled in my gut. The first potion worked. The second potion had to work on me too.

Glancing at the bars of my cell, I realized I could easily slip through. My chin dropped. I should've put the second potion on the other side of the bars. I'd be able to grow, access my magic, and be closer to the stairs.

Too late to change the plan now.

Scooting through the rat hole, I got a glimpse behind the walls of our house. It was dark. Dust rose from the concrete floor. Wood beams criss-crossed beneath the low hanging roof.

The second potion bottle glimmered in the light beside my sister's compact mirror. If I drank it here, I'd hit the ceiling, get stuck, and the noise would warn my family that something was afoot. I needed more space. Placing my hands on glass bottle, which was now taller than me, I pushed.

The bottle didn't move.

My shoulders slumped. I hadn't thought about being too small to move the bottle.

I pushed again. The potion wobbled.

Rushing to the other side, I held the bottle steady. The glass couldn't break or the potion would slush out. I'd be stuck as mini-me forever. I leaned against the bottle. What could I do?

A shuffling, sniffing reached my ears.

I froze.

A rat's beady eyes lit up the darkness.

My pulse raced. The rat I'd used as a guinea pig. The rat I could've killed. The rat who probably hated me and could now eat me. The acid in my stomach bubbled and swished. I held up my hands trying to show that I meant no harm and I hoped he didn't either.

"Hello, Mr. Rat. How are you feeling? You look great." Fear made my mouth spew words. "Better than great."

His whiskers twitched and he continued to stare. He was several inches bigger than me.

I swallowed. "I'm sorry I tried the potions on you." I raised my hands higher, "I used the first potion on myself."

The rat quirked his head. I didn't know if he understood or just listened to my voice. Maybe if I kept talking in a soothing tone he wouldn't attack.

"Unfortunately, I can't drink the second potion to get big again." I patted the potion bottle. "If I drink it here, I'd get stuck in this small pace and alert my family. And I can't push it somewhere else because it's too big. It's quite the dilemma."

My mind twirled, not seeing many options. I should've put the second potion into several smaller bottles. I sunk onto the ground and held my head in my hands. My eyes prickled. I refused to cry. But I didn't know what to do.

"I'm sorry I'm in your space. Is your home nearby?" Sniffling, I watched the rodent. He hadn't moved, seemingly more curious than antagonistic so I kept talking. "My family imprisoned me and I can't use magic in the basement. I needed to get out to warn my friends. Do you have friends, Mr. Rat?"

He angled his head the other way, appearing bigger and more intimidating.

Taking in his height, I remembered how he'd grown taller than the line I'd drawn on the crate. "Do you enjoy being a little bigger than you were before?"

I hated being smaller. I mean, I'm glad I was out of my prison but being little brought additional dangers, like Mr. Rat. It also brought memories of being the smallest kid at school. The other kids had picked on me. Jinx had made fun of me. At fifteen, I'd overtaken her in height and yet she still called me a baby.

The rat squeaked.

I cringed. What I would've been unable to hear as a regular-sized person sounded loud now. I gritted my teeth and huddled into a fetal position. I was going to be attacked by a rat.

Scuffling and shuffling caught my attention.

A second rat joined the first.

My ribcage squeezed tight. I was going to be attacked and eaten by two rats. Torn into bits and pieces. The images carved into my brain.

The second rat pressed its nose against Mr. Rat's. The whiskers shifted. It was similar to a kiss. Were they a couple? They targeted their gazes on me.

Stilling, I didn't know what to do. They were bigger and had sharp teeth. I had no weapon and no clothes.

The two rats advanced toward me.

I used my feet to shuffle backwards and came up against the wall. I had nowhere to go. I was going to die and would never be able to tell Lukas it wasn't me who kissed him, never say goodbye to my friends, never be able to warn them they were in danger. I'd disappear. Kind of like how I'd been invisible my entire life. Maybe they wouldn't even notice I was gone.

Mr. Rat's whiskers tickled my cheek.

I didn't laugh. Being gnawed on by two rats would be torture compared to drinking the potion.

"Mr. Rat, I don't taste good." I spouted stupid, terrified excuses. Anything to stop him from attacking.

He shifted toward the potion. His friend joined him. Standing on their hind legs, they placed their front paws on the bottle.

"No!" I jumped to my feet. They couldn't break the bottle. "I need the potion to get big again. You remember, Mr. Rat? The second drink made you big again. Bigger." I added a pleading tone.

The rats started pushing.

My eyes grew as large as the bottle. They weren't breaking or taking it. They were pushing it. They weren't going to eat me. They were helping.

My chest lightened and a smile burst on my face. "Oh my stars!" I pressed my palms together in praise. "Thank you! Thank you so much!"

The rats pushed the bottle under a wooden beam and through a tunnel of some sort. They followed a white pipe zigzagging through the small space.

"Do you know where you're going? Of course, you know." I flailed my hand. "You probably travel through the interior of the house all the time. Remember, I need a space big enough to grow." Following their path, I didn't even know if they understood.

But they'd understood my need to relocate the potion. Unless they were taking it away from me.

No. Mr. Rat was a new friend. Maybe I'd done him a favor by making him a little bigger. He could impress the friend he was with or scare the more normal sized rats.

The rats stopped under the stairs. The stairs climbed up and with each step the area got bigger and bigger. The best part, one side was open so I could easily get out.

"You're brilliant." I wanted to kiss Mr. Rat and his friend. I settled for giving them both a hug. I studied the bottle that was bigger than me and had a cork on top. "How do I drink it?"

The rats moved into position. The second rat climbed up the bottle and used her teeth and paws to remove the cork. She scrambled down and laid low next to it. Mr. Rat stood even taller and pushed the top of the bottle.

The potion sloshed inside and the bottle tipped.

"No!" I needed the potion.

Mr. Rat's friend caught the bottle as it tilted and rested the glass on its back. The bottle now lay at an angle with the top at a lower spot.

With pulse racing, I jumped up and tried to grab the edge. I still couldn't reach it.

Mr. Rat scrambled around to my side and laid flat on his stomach.

Squinting at the top of the tilted bottle and my new friend, I wasn't sure what he wanted. Did he want a sip of the potion so he'd become giant? Not going to happen. I refused to be responsible for a giant rat let loose in the coven.

He shimmied his body and I finally understood. I climbed onto his back, balanced myself, and stood. I could now touch the open top and drink.

No time to think or worry, I swallowed the potion with greed. I never wanted to be small again. It was too scary and too hard to get places.

The liquid didn't burn down my throat. Instead, ice scraped into my chest. I had a hard time breathing because my lungs became encased in ice. The ice slid further into my system and I shivered.

My insides went frigid. My bloodstream chilled from within. My arms and legs went numb.

My mind went numb. What if I froze to death?

My trembling skin stretched, each limb being pulled in a vice. My bones cracked and grew and mended again. My legs sprawled like spiders. My arms sprouted and lengthened. Agony speared through my temple with the worst brain freeze ever.

I tumbled off Mr. Rat's back and landed hard on the ground. I was so frigid, I'm surprised my body didn't crack like ice.

The washcloth shrunk, or I should say, *I grew.*

And grew and grew and grew.

My head hit beneath the stairs. I was big and naked again. My cheeks warmed.

Crossing my arms, I smiled at Mr. Rat and his friend. "Thank you so much. You saved my life."

Mr. Rat saluted me with his tiny paw and both rats scurried away. Mr. Rat returned carrying my sister's compact.

"Thank you!" The compact could come in handy because of its magic.

He waved again and left.

I was free. Well, at least partially.

I couldn't apparate from inside because my parents had locked our home down once Jinx started getting into trouble with boys. I also didn't want to land somewhere without clothes. Which meant going upstairs, finding clothes, and getting out.

Crouching lower, I crawled through the opening on the other side of the stairs into the non-potion cellar side of the basement. I quickly searched for clothes to wear but found nothing. Silently, I climbed the stairs while nerves tapped in my chest.

When I arrived at the top, I cracked the door and stuck the mirror around the corner to see if anyone was around. The hallway was empty and I sagged with relief. I tiptoed into the hall and took a quick right at the mudroom.

The mudroom was filled with shoes and boots and even a pile of clothes. I released the breath I didn't know I'd been holding. I could get dressed. Rummaging through the pile, I found clothes from my much larger dad, my tiny mom, and my sister. Nothing of mine.

A sign of what they planned to do with me when this ended perhaps? Did they plan to make me disappear permanently?

Ha. I'd foiled the plot.

Grabbing a pair of my sister's jeans, I slipped them on and put the mirror in the pocket. The jeans were too short, shorter than Jinx's clothes would normally be on me. I picked the first top off the pile and pulled it over my head and slipped on a pair of too tight black boots.

Facing the mirror, I examined myself. My face appeared the same, the banshee mark blaring on my forehead. My green hair appeared lighter. Had the transformation lightened the natural color? The black halter top had a deep plunge in the center and circular open rivets revealing skin. The jeans were so short they resembled capris. I'd gotten taller.

Footsteps came down the hall. "Jinx, is that you?"

My stomach clutched. My mom. I'd taken too long.

I dashed toward the back door and wrapped my fingers around the doorknob. Twisting, I pulled. Nothing budged. My heart stopped.

The door was locked.

Chapter Five

Internally, I shrieked. After what I'd gone through to get out, I couldn't be stopped by a stupid locked door. Wrapping my hand around the knob tighter, I shook the handle.

"Jinx?" My mother called again, timid and unsure. Her steps came closer. "We really need to talk about—"

I didn't want to hear anything she wanted to talk about with my sister. I wanted her to want to talk to me, to be with me. The urge to run into her arms flooded through me. She'd once loved me. Hadn't she? Doubts jammed the tide of emotion. Her recent actions proved her loyalties. I had to get out. I didn't want my mother to use her magic against me, proving once and for all that she was against me.

My brain stuttered. Her magic.

If she had magic, I had magic. My fingers tingled and I pointed at the door. "*Reserare*. Unlock."

The door clicked.

Euphoria rushed through my veins and sprinkled my skin. My magic was back. I turned the handle, opened the door, and hurried out, closing the door quietly behind me. Galloping, I dashed around the side of the house and hid behind a bush in our small yard. I bent at the waist and breathed clean, fresh, free air.

"What next?" I had to find Destiny. She was at the center of whatever sinister scheme Jinx worked on with Mistress Lita. "*Locatus* Destiny." I focused on my friend's essence, trying to locate her. "Take me there."

I apparated out and landed in a room in the tower of the Inferis Coven Academy.

What would I do without magic? I wouldn't survive long term that's for sure. It had been difficult with limited magic at the banshee encampment and under the human palace, especially when I was mining. And don't forget, just now, while locked in the potion cellar.

A flash scorched my chest which I quickly squashed. Anger wouldn't help me now. I'd unpack my emotions about my family later.

Standing behind a large wardrobe, I heard talking and peeked further into the room.

The pentagon shaped room had circular windows on every wall. A French door led out to a balcony and a huge bed dominated the room. Destiny had been given one of the best rooms in the academy. Why?

It didn't matter now. What mattered was the people in the room.

Destiny, Stone, and Jinx—resembling me, stood in the center of the room. She wore the dress she'd had on earlier. Destiny wore simple leggings and a black shirt. She appeared to be dressed for a clandestine mission, not a romantic moment with her boyfriend. Stone was dressed in a formal human suit. How had he gotten past the wards and enchantments keeping non-witches out of the academy? I bet Jinx and Mistress Lita had something to do with his presence.

Nerves quivered along my spine. I couldn't jump out and announce myself because Jinx might hurt my friends. Plus, my friends might believe her instead of me, especially since I'd gotten taller. They'd spent the last several days with her as she pretended to be me. I needed to be patient, to watch and listen and learn.

"I'm saying you should stay at the Inferis Coven and become leader. We're too different and you're too powerful. We're over, Destiny." Stone's stiff delivery told me something was wrong.

Destiny froze. Her expression blanked as if she was numb or unable to process his declaration. Was he really breaking up with her?

Destiny and Stone were the perfect couple. If they didn't work out, who would? Certainly not Lukas and I, whom my sister had kissed. If we were meant to be together, shouldn't he have realized Jinx was an imposter? My heart squeezed. If Jinx's chemical signature had already impressed on Lukas, then he could be mated to her for life. That's what Jinx had hinted at when she'd bragged about kissing him.

Destiny glanced at her grandfather's watch. "We'll talk about this when I get back. Stay here." She raced from the room before I got the opportunity to talk to her.

I wanted to scream *wait* but knew I couldn't.

"Stay here." Jinx ordered Stone to stand in one place.

My brow furrowed. Why would he listen to her?

Jinx, looking like me, followed Destiny out the door.

My gut tightened. Should I stay put, follow my sister, or talk to Stone? He might know what was happening and be safer to approach.

I peeked out from behind the furniture. "Stone?" I ran to his side and shook him. He didn't blink. "Stone?"

He must be under a spell which meant he probably didn't want to break up with Destiny. I tapped my finger on my chin. I couldn't break a spell I didn't know.

"Human!" Jinx yelled from the hallway and her hurried footsteps came back toward the room.

Startled, I jumped and dashed back to my hiding spot.

Jinx stalked back into the room with a glower on *my* face. "Destiny is a stubborn girl. I couldn't convince her to agree." My sister frowned and patted his cheek. "Don't worry, Stone. I'll get you back to your palace soon and you can go on with your dreary life for as long as Mistress Lita allows you and that naive King Zacharye." Jinx chuckled. "Before the mistress and I take control of the entire kingdom."

Darkness roiled my brain. Jinx's plot involved the entire Kingdom of Alandaska. This was big. She was working with Mistress Lita and they needed Destiny to do something. But what?

Was this too big for me to handle? I didn't know who I could trust at the coven or how to find my other friends. I had to get more information.

"First, I need to help Mistress Lita get your girlfriend—I mean *ex*-girl-friend—to do what she wants, beginning with making her feel despair about your breakup." Jinx ran her fingers across Stone's cheek.

He didn't flinch.

She stilled, glanced up, and smirked. "My familiar tells me Destiny is at the Subterrane Abyss cavern. Why? It's not time for the Ascension Ceremony yet."

Jinx was as slimy as her snake familiar. She knew I hated snakes. If I didn't know the familiar picked the witch, I would've thought she'd done it on purpose to annoy me.

"I'll send a message to Mistress Lita and we'll be on the way." Jinx's cruel laughter echoed through the room, giving me chills. "I think right before we send Destiny to the Underworld we should engage in the most romantic kiss. Send her to *helvete* heartbroken that her best friend stole her boyfriend. She deserves it for the trouble she's caused me."

It felt as if a boiling, black cauldron dropped into my center. While pretending to be me, my sister had kissed Lukas and now she planned to kiss Stone. She wanted to hurt Destiny in more ways than one and she was using me to make it worse.

Jinx snapped her fingers and chains appeared around Stone's wrists and ankles. She strutted out the door, and Stone robotically followed her.

The muscles in my face hardened and my jaw went rigid. I couldn't let Jinx use my likeness to be so cruel. I had to learn what she was up to and how it involved my friends. Using an invisibility spell, I followed them through the academy and outside to Dark Angel's Veil.

I shivered. This was the waterfall where young witches had been kidnapped and dragged into the river by the Dark Angel. I halted. Mom had mumbled something about fearing the Underworld. Why was Jinx going near? Did she have a deal with the devil?

Sagging against a boulder, I caught my breath. I didn't know what to do. I wanted to help. But what could I do against my powerful sister and Mistress Lita?

I could warn my friends and they'd come up with a plan. I could be the sidekick as always. Determination rammed through me and I straightened. What I was, hero or helper, shouldn't matter. I needed to do something.

Jinx and Stone continued between two large boulders and into a cave near the waterfall. They disappeared into the darkness.

I pushed off and followed the trail between the boulders. Dark and damp hit me like a wall. "*Lux.*" A lighted sphere snapped in the palm of my hand.

The light didn't help me see much more. Boulders were in front of and behind me. Cracks large enough for Jinx and Stone to slip through appeared between every surface.

My belly fluttered. I had no clue which way they went.

Shimmying through a crack, I peeked in and tried to distinguish if they'd gone this way. Nothing.

I went through a second crack and a third. On the fourth crack, which was a little wider than the others, I spotted a muddy, large footprint. Stone's.

They'd gone this way. I followed the path until I heard voices and dimmed my light.

"Punishment for your crimes will be severe." Mistress Lita's harshness cut through my confusion.

Picking up a hefty rock, I edged forward and hid behind a stalagmite. I could use the rock as a weapon or throw it to cause a distraction.

Destiny faced Mistress Lita across the grotto. Jinx stood near the mistress, slightly to the side. Stone waited between the two of them. Behind Destiny stood Damien, Xenos, and Ulrich, warlocks from the academy. Melancholy swept through me. Destiny had made new friends.

"Oh, like spending the rest of my life on the banks of the River Styx?" Destiny jutted her hip.

I perked forgetting my melancholy. The only one who spent their life on the banks of the River Styx was the Dark Angel.

"I spoke with the Dark Angel and I know *everything*." Destiny spoke with such assurance. She must have a plan to thwart the mistress.

Relieved, I let my shoulders droop. Destiny always had a plan. Which was good, right? She had confidence and strength, plus her combined banshee and witch magic. Wishing I had confidence or more powerful magic, I shrunk in stature, similar to when I'd drank the Accipere Parvus potion. If Destiny had a plan, I couldn't overreact. I might blow whatever scheme she had cooked up.

I scanned the area. Stalactites and stalagmites pointed up and down as if confused about which direction to go. They crowded the area especially with all the people in the cavern. Who was on Destiny's side for real and who was pretending? I had to be ready to jump in to assist. And where was Lukas?

The ground shook and I fell forward. I dropped the rock and grabbed onto the stalagmite to stay standing. I couldn't reveal myself yet. The others stumbled and ducked. With the noise of falling rocks, I couldn't hear the discussion.

Mistress Lita's evil laughter sent a shudder down my spine. She raised her wand and screamed in Latin something about *bringing her a life source.*

An orange glowing ball leapt off her wand, whirling and spinning. A strong spell of fire. Ripples streamed out in waves, destroying everything solid in its path. The ball roared toward Destiny.

Destiny pulled out the famous Obsidian's Fire wand and the orange ball stopped moving toward her. She definitely had a plan, and with the powerful wand in her possession, she'd be able to make it work.

A plan I wasn't involved in.

Dispirited, I rocked back on my feet. Even when we escaped the banshees, my role had been minor. She was the real hero. Not me.

The ball of fire unwound and went in the opposite direction, toward Mistress Lita and my sister, standing beside her. The powerful ball would devour them both. The mistress' gaze went wide, clearly surprised at what Destiny had done. Jinx's, or should I say *my,* expression was blank. She must not realize what was about to happen.

I leaned forward as nerves raced across my skin. Tension threaded through me.

No matter how much trouble she'd caused she was still my sister. If I was about to go to purgatory she'd save me, wouldn't she? Sure, she'd locked me up and been led astray by the power Mistress Lita dangled before her, but I couldn't watch her die. I could save her, expose her, and be the hero.

Mistress Lita should go to the Underworld. Jinx could pay for her crimes in a different way.

My shoulders straightened as determination set in my bones. I'd save her and help Destiny. I'd finally be a champion in my own right.

I rushed forward as the orange ball surrounded Jinx and Mistress Lita. If anyone noticed me, they didn't have time to react. I placed my hands on my sister's back and pushed her out of the way. She stumbled forward and fell to the ground.

The orange ball engulfed Mistress Lita and me. Heat seared, worse than drinking the Get Small potion. The magical flame consumed me, making me so hot that I shivered. Tormented waves of incineration lit me on fire.

Gloom became my smoke in the fire. I'd be burned to a crisp. Die and be unrecognizable.

Jinx swiveled around exhibiting wide eyes and a pale face. Her shocked expression told me I'd done the right thing. I'd saved her. Her lips twisted upwards, and wearing *my* smile, she sent a final sinister grin.

Chapter Six

And I fell.

Fell through the Archeron Barrier and into the Underworld.

Chapter Seven

"Did you hear me, Cassia?" The hot guy grabbed my hand and pulled me back into my current predicament.

My new reality. I'd fallen to the Underworld, been attacked by a cerberus, and kissed by an angel. A Dark Angel. All of what came before this awful moment wouldn't save me or help me escape.

"You're here for good, Cassia. You're not leaving now or ever." Had he read my mind?

Who was he to be telling me how the rest of my life would end? Just because he swooped down and kissed me, just because he said he was the son of the Dark Angel, and just because he seemed to be the only person on the banks of the River Styx, did not mean I'd go along with his plan or his kisses.

"No." I scrambled to my feet while anxiety rolled in my stomach and torment weighed heavy in my chest. "I won't stay."

I revolved toward the rock wall. Shoving my hands into crevices, I climbed. Almost instantly, I slid back to the ground. I repeated the action, refusing to give up. I had no magic to assist me.

"You don't have a choice. I'm Onyx." The name fit.

He was dark, cool, mysterious, and exhibited a stone hard expression. He believed I couldn't leave the banks of the River Styx. But he didn't know my friends.

I slid to the ground again and my eyes burned.

He held out a strong hand with slender fingers and clipped nails. "And you are?"

A failure.

And he'd already called me by my name.

Hunching my shoulders, I refused to shake his hand. This wasn't a social meeting. There was nothing normal about this situation. I heaved again. I was alive and yet stuck on the banks of the River Styx. Panic shot higher and I panted a couple of times. "I won't be here long. My friends will rescue me."

"What should I call you until your friends arrive?" His lips twitched. He didn't believe me.

"You already said my name." I spit out, both to get him off my back and because I couldn't breathe. Maybe I needed another kiss. No. "And you don't know my friends. Destiny has spoken with the Dark Angel. She has unusual powers."

Onyx glared. The twitch in his lips flattened into a straight line. "My father's great granddaughter."

Hope lightened in my chest. "You know her?"

"I've heard stories about her." His hardness sounded hateful. "My father was so proud of her."

He seemed jealous of Destiny, similar to how I'd always felt about Jinx. We had something in common. One thing in common. He was from the Underworld and I was a good witch. I wouldn't end up in purgatory.

The cerberus returned, chewed on the bone, and dropped it at my feet.

I wasn't going to touch it. "Go away, Cerb."

The three-headed dog disappeared except for three sets of sharp teeth.

I jerked back. The animal had become invisible apart from his mouth. How was that possible? Cerb must have dark magic too.

"My father boasted that Destiny will be the greatest witch ever." Onyx's sour tone tried to show he didn't care. I could tell he did. "She'll either lead the Inferis Coven or the undead to greatness. Her powers are combined."

Destiny would be great and Onyx wasn't happy about the situation. Maybe he didn't appreciate the spotlight being hogged. She didn't do it on purpose. "She is great. She defeated Mistress Lita and sent her down here."

"She sent you down here too." His words stabbed because it hadn't been Destiny's betrayal.

I'd chosen to save my ungrateful sister.

"I have combined powers too. Warlock and Dark Angel," Onyx bragged.

If he was the new Dark Angel, he had dark magic. "You could send me back."

"No." His expression stayed flat, harsh and uncompromising.

"Why not?" I let my scared emotions out in a screech.

Pivoting, he started to saunter away. "Come on, boy."

Cerb didn't move, or at least his teeth didn't. The animal stayed by my side.

I watched Onyx leave. My pulse charged wanting to follow him. I didn't want to be in this creepy place scared and alone. I didn't like him but at least he was company. Plus, he knew things about this place.

"Wait!" I jogged after him. "Why won't you help me?"

Cerb reappeared by his side with the bone in his mouth. He chomped on it as he trotted beside me. His heavy steps pounded on the dry ground.

"Drop it, Cerb." Onyx bent down to pick up the bone exhibiting his nice butt in those black leather pants.

Not that I was looking.

His leather vest cinched in at the waist emphasizing his broad shoulders and strong chest. The black T-shirt tugged on his arms displaying powerful biceps.

Okay, maybe I was looking.

He tossed the bone and the dog ran after it. He continued to saunter forward as though he didn't have a care in the world. Leaving me behind.

Shaking my head, I was flummoxed. This place was a weird wonderland where everything was backwards. An unwelcoming atmosphere where I needed to be kissed to breathe. A three-headed animal behaving like a puppy. A hot teen guy acting tough and hard, yet he cared about his pet.

"How old are you?"

He didn't answer at first, just turned around and stared at me with deep soulless eyes. "Seventeen. How old are you?"

My heart stuttered. He was about the same age as me. "Sixteen. Destiny turned seventeen at midnight, and she's your father's great granddaughter. Are you her uncle?"

"Our only connection is my father." Onyx sounded caustic about the fact.

Cerb became visible in front of me and dropped the bone.

I ignored the dog.

Onyx scratched the dog on one of its heads. "It's after midnight. We need to get home. Come on, Cerb."

My brain rattled. Did that mean he was going to send me home? Or were he and his dog going home to wherever they lived?

Onyx started walking. Cerb stayed by me even though I didn't want him by my side.

"Are you coming?" Onyx glanced back at me.

"Where?" I didn't want to go anywhere with him. But I also didn't want to be left alone.

"Are you planning to spend the night on the banks of the river?" He waved his arm indicating the river flowing in front of us.

The water flowed swiftly. If someone fell in, they'd drown.

I looked away not wanting to think about death. But in my current environment, how could I not? "Do you have a curfew or something?"

When I'd followed my sister to the cavern called the Subterrane Abyss, it had been right around midnight, almost Destiny's birthday. By now it must be the middle of the night.

"No. It's not safe to be out on the banks this late."

Shivering, I crossed my arms. He was trying to scare me even more, and it was working. "Isn't it just the two of us?"

"The only two majiks." His lips shifted to sly and secretive before he turned away and started moving again. "Suit yourself."

I froze even in the sultry environment. He wasn't going to try to convince me. He'd let me stay out here alone and defenseless.

"It will be a shame if something happens to you." Whistling, he kept walking.

His tight leather pants hugged his hips and muscular thighs as he sauntered away. He stood tall and proud, displaying strong, wide shoulders. Squeezing my eyes closed for a second, I shouldn't notice his attractiveness. I was in peril. If I left this area, Destiny would never find me.

"What do you mean by something happening to me?" My voice trembled.

His broad shoulders shrugged. He didn't stop.

I darted toward him and grabbed his arm. Heat emanated through his T-shirt, warming me internally. "What do you mean?"

His blasé expression must be a mask. He knew something. "My mother told me tales about the undead when I was a kid."

The word *undead* struck a sharp pang. What did he mean by that? "And you always do what your mother says."

A cruel tease but he made me angry.

"My mother's tales were vivid and violent." For a second he resembled a scared little boy that I wanted to help, and then everything on his face went hard again.

Or maybe he wanted me to empathize with him. "What did your father say?"

"Not much." Onyx's curtness showed no emotion. "As long as I listened to his commands, I was okay."

Meaning his father wouldn't hurt him? I cringed at the suggestion of abuse.

His shoulders straightened and he became the in-charge guy again. "And those commands from my mother and father include that I be home by midnight, and it's well after now."

"Your father's gone. Why are you still listening to him?"

Creepy, bone-chilling howls erupted.

Startled, my heartrate spiked and I stepped closer to his side.

"That's why." He took hold of my hand and tugged me along.

In a daze, I let him pull me. Obviously, Destiny wasn't going to save me this second. I needed to stay somewhere safe during the witching hours—or the creepy scream hours. When she came, I'd leave with her. Except, when I'd been trapped in the basement she'd never come, although she didn't realize I was missing. This time she would.

I hoped.

Decision made, I clung to his hand. "Okay. I'll come with you but I'm only staying for one night."

As we walked, my eyes must've finally adjusted to the darkness. The land we crossed was barren except for the muddy river we followed. Every once in a while I swear something peeked out from the water. I didn't ask until I spotted several snouts.

I tripped on a rock and his hand tightened around mine, keeping me upright. "What was that?"

"What?"

"The thing in the river?" My voice rose higher.

"Never go in the river."

I huffed. "Another rule?"

"Rules are how you survive the harsh environment." He had no sympathy.

Still holding my hand, he slid between two cliffs with sheer faces. The path between the two boulders was wet like clay as if a stream had recently retreated. "Welcome to your new home."

I stopped, taking in the building in front of me.

Faded red paint covered most of the exterior of the house. Small spade-shaped windows punctuated the red with darkness. A shabby railing hung around a front porch, and I couldn't tell if the house was one story or three. The building disappeared into the black sky above.

"Not my home." I followed him through the squeaky front door.

Lights burst to life in the interior and I gaped at the mess. Messier than my parents' home. The tiny entryway with black and white checked flooring led right into the living room. A bright purple couch was surrounded by mushroom shaped chairs patterned with spades, diamonds, clovers, and hearts as decoration. One of the chairs was broken and balanced on its side. Other broken furniture was piled in the corner. Various clocks hung on the walls. One crazy clock had multiple hands shaped like arm and finger bones. The hands swung around to a different time frame than reality.

"What is that mark?" Onyx rubbed his thumb across my forehead.

A tingle spread and heated my skin. He must not have noticed the banshee mark in the dark outside. I lifted my chin, forgetting his interesting decor. He hadn't noticed my appearance until we'd entered a lighted space. Which was probably a good thing because after being locked in the family basement for days I'm sure I looked a mess.

"It's a tattoo." I wasn't going to tell him my entire saga.

"Cool." He lifted his black T-shirt revealing his sculpted abs and chest. "I have a tattoo too."

Black wings spread from the tip of one broad shoulder to the other and in the center were four playing cards. The four cards displayed each of the suits: diamond, heart, spade, and the clover on top. And a skull in the middle.

It was intricate and beautiful, and I was drawn to the image.

On its own, my hand reached up to touch the tattoo.

The cards shuffled on his chest and the card with the heart landed on top.

My eyes widened and I jerked my hand back. "What just happened to your tattoo?"

"It's magical just like me." He took off his shirt completely and flexed his arm muscles.

I closed my eyes and shook my head, not sure I'd believed what I saw. "Does it hurt when it changes?"

"No." He tossed the shirt onto the floor, and shrugged. "The house needs a woman's touch."

A servant more like.

I huffed. "And you think I should clean because I'm a girl?"

"No, because *I'm* the Dark Angel." He glanced away, possibly embarrassed by the mess or his chauvinistic attitude. He picked up a dirty teacup. "It needs your touch."

I halted my inspection of his naked chest and shook my head. "I'm not staying."

The kitchen held a small wood table with a bowl of strange orange fruit. Two chairs with spindly legs and decorative designs surrounded the table. Again, black and white checks, brightly colored spades, diamonds, clovers, and hearts. A pile of what I thought was kindling sat in the corner, until I noticed the wood was decorated the same as the chairs. A bright red teapot sat on the stove and colorful teacups lined one shelf. If Onyx decorated this house, I'd be shocked.

He grabbed my hand and yanked me against him. "You will stay and be my Red Queen."

I choked. "What's a Red Queen?"

"It's what my mother was to the old Dark Angel." Onyx's expression softened, remembering good times.

My brow furrowed. "I thought you said your mother was a kidnapped witch."

I didn't want the same fate. Forced to stay and have a child, trapped in the Underworld like Onyx. I wanted to go back to the coven.

"My mother loved my father and was obedient to him until the day she died." He made it seem like his mother could do no wrong. He had a soft spot for her, had put her on a pedestal, the opposite of me and my mother. "Even though my father loved another."

Mistress Lita. She'd put off death for decades and finally been forced to the Underworld by Destiny. I'd seen the mistress fall. That must've been when Onyx's father died and together, the old Dark Angel and Mistress Lita had traveled down the River Styx to their final destination.

Bending down, Onyx's mouth captured mine with punishing force. Shocked, I couldn't react. He moved my palm against his bare chest and I felt his heart beating at a fast pace. My heart joined with his in the same rhythm, calming my initial rejection and soothing my soul.

Wrapping his other arm around my back, he pressed me closer. The warmth of his body seeped into my skin and I fought against this magnetic pull he had on me.

I refused to be conquered.

Keeping my mouth closed and stiff, I tried to twist away in his arms.

He held me tight, while his hard lips mellowed as he teased and cajoled. The kiss went from threatening to enjoyable.

My heart raced to keep up pace with his. What kind of magic was this?

My mouth opened of its own volition and his tongue swept inside. Our tongues tangled and I didn't want to stop. The kiss turned mutual. Our mouths were made for each other.

He broke off the kiss and grinned, a sexy confident smirk.

My body went weak, but I straightened my knees and tried to stand on my own. "Are you kissing me so I can breathe?"

If so, why was I so breathless?

"No, that wasn't the Kiss of Afterlife. I just wanted to kiss you." His smile twitched and then hardened. His obsidian eyes narrowed and he captured me with his gaze. "Take note. The only difference between our relationship and my mother and father's is, *you* will love me."

He believed he'd already won.

His attitude had me straightening my posture. I wouldn't do what he wanted or listen to his stupid rules. I'd been an idiot believing my sister and family had missed me. I wouldn't be gullible again.

I took a step back. "Are you mad? I will not stay and be your queen of coffins or queen of the Underworld. I will not stay in purgatory."

"You will stay." His harshness scraped against my spine and bruised my heart. "You will be *my* Red Queen. But never forget, I will be the one in charge."

Chapter Eight

I rolled over and fell off the couch onto the dirty rug. "Ouch."

A big bundle of fur snored. Cerb. The dog had slept on the floor beside the couch, taking up all the space on the floor. He was probably guarding me, making sure I didn't leave. Luckily I didn't fall on him.

Rubbing my eyes, I glanced around. I was in Onyx's house on the banks of the River Styx. I'd been hoping it was a nightmare—including the argument I'd had with the master of the house.

Last night, I'd told him I was tired and asked where I could sleep. He'd opened the door to his bedroom. "My bed is comfy." He'd wiggled his eyebrows in a suggestive manner.

"No chance." I'd been breathless again, wondering if I needed another Kiss of Afterlife. But that was the last thing I'd suggest at this moment. It was too similar to the real kiss and gave me strange feelings I'd never had before. "I'm not sharing a bed with you."

"Suit yourself. There's the couch. I slept on it for years." He'd entered the bedroom and slammed the door behind him.

Onyx was no gentleman.

Not that I'd met many gentlemen. My father wasn't a gentleman or he wouldn't have locked me in the basement. The warlocks at the coven pretended to be nice but always had an ulterior motive. Only Lukas had helped and defended me, until he became bonded with my sister. A sad tune played in my head.

Watching Cerb curled up against the furniture with his feet in the air, I smiled. I'd always wanted a dog, and asleep, he appeared soft and cuddly. Still, if he woke up he'd probably warn Onyx of my departure.

Standing, I brushed off my sister's tight jeans and shirt. Onyx probably wanted to sleep with me because of my revealing clothes. Typical man. Plus, I was the only girl available down here. His existence must be lonely. Shaking off any empathy, I had to leave. I had to go back to the place I'd landed so my friends could find me.

One of the many boney hour hands on the crazy clock swung around and stopped at the six. It had to be morning, even though I didn't believe the timepiece was accurate. I'd slept like the dead. I hoped that didn't mean anything.

Bending down, I slipped on my boots and tiptoed so as not to wake Cerb. Tension threaded through my muscles and bones. I needed to be extra quiet. I stepped to the door and twisted the knob. It moved. The door wasn't locked. Interesting Onyx brought me here but didn't lock me inside. I relaxed. Maybe he didn't mean to keep me captive. Maybe he thought he could charm me into staying.

Turning around, I gently closed the door behind me. The sulfur smell made me gasp and I choked. The sky had lightened a little. It must always be a certain level of dark. I could never get used to the gloom.

Sailing forward, my feet squelched in the mud. Puddles of water steamed. I skipped over the puddles and slipped between the two rock cliffs we'd come through last night. My mouth dropped open.

The river had come up and over the banks. Large swells lapped close to my feet. I took a step back. It was how the river in the coven—the Helvete River—looked right after a storm. Water rushed and gurgled and roared.

The River Styx was no longer flowing and peaceful. The river was a water highway to hades.

A huge wave rolled out from the middle and crashed against the two cliff-like boulders I stood between. The path we'd taken last night to Onyx's house. Water reached my feet and pants.

"Oof." The water sizzled. I shook my arms and jumped onto a rock set against one of the boulders. I refused to run back to the house. My body trembled even though the water was hot. I was stuck on this high spot of land until the river subsided, otherwise I could drown.

The wave continued past me and stopped short of his door.

Maybe it wasn't the boulders protecting his house but some kind of magic. Elemental or dark magic.

Another wave crashed against the large boulder, right where I stood.

"Ah!" I stumbled and stuck my arms out toward the boulder, trying to keep my footing. Panic ratcheted up resembling the water. Both directions were blocked. I couldn't go forward or back. Water surrounded me. My lungs emptied, which was bad because if I fell in the river, I'd need all the oxygen I could get.

A fish stuck its head out of the water. Creepy green and black eyes. Long pointy teeth overlapping the jawline. I sucked in a breath. This is what I'd seen last night.

My pulse jittered and I scrambled up the cliff wall trying to get a grip. Lifting my legs, I tried to stay out of the water.

Cerb barked. A cerberus could take on this weird fish.

"Cerb! Over here!" Screaming for him, the opposite of how I'd treated him last night, I hoped the dog could save me.

My dangling body swung with the next wave and my fingers cramped. I wouldn't be able to hold on much longer. My ribs constricted and I gasped. I was going to fall into the river and either boil to death or be eaten by the weird fish. Or I'd float down the River Styx before actually dying.

Another fish reared its ugly head. The fish stayed in the spot right by my dangling feet waiting for me to fall. They both chomped their teeth.

Hysteria rose, picturing those teeth gnawing through my skin. If I fell, I'd sink. I did not want to be their breakfast. "Cerb!"

He barked again and flames shot out of his three mouths aimed at me. Or was he trying to fry the fish? How could he be thinking about eating right now? "Cerb!"

"Cassia!" Onyx rushed out of the house leaving the door open. "Cassia!"

He actually sounded worried about me and my insides softened. He'd come to the rescue again. But because he cared or because he wanted me to stay with him? Everything inside hardened. I couldn't owe him for the rescue, especially not owe him my life.

I might never have been the hero, but I always assisted in the rescue. But I didn't understand this environment and I needed help. No point in dying because of my pride.

"Onyx! Up here." I hung on. "Onyx!"

"Hold on." He stood just out of reach of the rising water and held out his hand with his palm facing toward me.

My brow scrunched. What was he doing?

Red, orange, and yellow spirals of light swirled from Onyx's palm. The spirals curved and swerved and dipped into the water. The brown muddy river lit with a murky green color. The water roiled and bubbled.

My jaw dropped. Water was used to fight fire. So why not the opposite in a paradoxical place?

The water grew taller and gathered strength. The green water whirled in a waterspout with the colors of fire. The spout charged in my direction.

My eyes widened and my pulse shrieked. The water rolled toward me in a large, colorful wave. He manipulated the water. He'd called the wave. Did he want to kill me?

The wave bashed into me. My cheek hit the side of the cliff and I felt dizzy. I lost my grip and fell into the water. All the air left my lungs. Onyx was trying to drown me or serve me up on a platter for the monster fish.

The water curled around me. Sputtering, I swung my arms trying to get away from the wave and above the surface. My body was flotsam, floating in the direction the wave wanted me to go. I had no control—story of my life.

No control of my upbringing. My childhood was centered around Jinx. No control while in prison. The human guards tortured us. No control once I returned.

Swinging my head, I tried to spot the strange fish and saw nothing. My body hit something hard and warm. The wave swept away and I found myself in Onyx's arms. I clung to him, gasping for air and holding on for life. He held me snug, afraid I might be snatched away by another rogue wave.

My head cradled into his shoulder. My long hair and wet clothes dripped onto his strong dry body. His earthy scent infiltrated my senses and real-ization slapped me. "I could've died."

"How convenient since you were in the River Styx." His cold callousness chafed against my confusion. Fear still pulsed through me.

I slapped his bare chest with the cards and wings tattoo and my hand stung. "I could've drowned." Because of his rogue wave.

The cards in the deck shuffled and the heart card laid on top.

"You're welcome." His smarmy smirk set me off.

"I said I could've drowned *because* of you." I throttled the words like I wanted to throttle him.

"You didn't. I know how to control my powers." Superior smugness radiated off him and I wished I was that assured of my own magic.

He'd used dark magic to make a wave and controlled the water to lift and carry me to his arms. What else could he do? I bet he could send me home. I had to convince him.

Another wave came in and soaked his feet. Cerb trotted back inside the house.

"We should go inside." Onyx carried me over the threshold and kicked the door closed, unknowingly enacting the human post-marriage ritual.

I gulped. "Why was the river so high?"

He tossed me onto the couch, uncaring that I got the cushions wet. The forcefulness of the throw displayed his anger. "Why did you sneak out?" His hard tone cut across any thoughts about marriage.

"I need to get back to where I landed." The desperation driving me returned. "When my friends arrive, I need to be there."

His gaze seared into mine and then traveled below my neck. Warmed by his glance, I shifted and looked down. The halter top clung to my breasts. Heat rose on my cheeks. I sat up straight and tugged the material away from my skin.

"Your friends are not coming." He stalked into the kitchen, picked up a tea towel, and threw it at me.

"They will come." I snatched the towel and wiped off my face and arms. "What happened to the river? It wasn't high last night."

"More die at night." He shrugged as if it was a normal occurrence. "Last night, more died than usual." His rough voice hinted at raw emotion. Nothing showed on his face.

I leaned forward, curious about him and his knowledge. "How do you know?"

His expression went pensive and when he finally spoke his tone filled with sadness. "I'm the Dark Angel."

My heart pounded. He was the opposite of Santa Claus. Onyx didn't know when people were good or bad. He knew when they died. The Dark

Angel assisted the dead on their passage. He was constantly surrounded by darkness and death. How did that warp a personality?

The urge to comfort him stirred inside. I tucked my hand under my wet jeans. "What happened in the kingdom?" Swallowing, I wasn't sure if I wanted to know. Mistress Lita was dead but Jinx had been involved in the plot to take over. She could cause mayhem on her own.

"It's confidential." He tilted his chin up and a slow smile dawned on his face. "I could tell you, if you become my Red Queen."

"No." Even though I knew sharing his burdens would lighten his load, I refused to become his queen.

But if not me, who?

A sliver of green entered my veins. I wasn't jealous. No one else lived down here anyway, unless he started kidnapping witches like his father.

"I quit putting up the dam walls to protect the house years ago because the river quit rising." He angled his head and his brow furrowed. "My father was worried that less people were dying."

"Which is odd because we've had a war in the kingdom." Although there'd also been major medical breakthroughs, and of course, magic to heal. "Will you tell me what those things are in the water at least? The fish with the sharp teeth."

"Ghoul fish. Stay away from those." He sounded more concerned than demanding. Leaning against the counter, he chuckled. "They're the reason the dead take a boat to their final destination."

Shivering, I didn't appreciate his dark humor.

"You're cold." He stepped away from the counter and sauntered toward his bedroom. "Take a bath."

I'd used the small bathroom off the kitchen last night, the one without a tub. Standing, I followed him to the edge of his room and pulled the wet top away from my body. "What about a change of clothes?"

"I can find you something." He stopped next to the big king-sized bed with a black bedspread crumpled at the foot. Black satin sheets lay on top. "Coming?"

He said it like a challenge. He believed I didn't have the courage to step into his room. Straightening my back, I edged in.

The far wall featured a built-in bookshelf crammed with different kinds of books. I recognized a witch spell book and a warlock guide. There was a book about dark magic and the Underworld. Fiction books took up a lot of the space. I noted some of my favorite classics by Charles Dickens, Tolkien, and even Bram Stoker. A wrought iron spiral staircase wound up into the ceiling.

He opened a door on the other side of the room, distracting me from the intriguing staircase. "In here."

This wall had two doors, one to the bathroom and the other possibly a closet. A heavy dresser filled the space between with a coffin shaped mirror. Not my style of decorating.

I followed him into the bathroom.

A claw footed copper tub took up most of the space in the room. It appeared unused. No water marks or stains. A small shower backed into the corner next to a pedestal sink. Another door led to the toilet. Partially burnt candles sat in every open space. I couldn't smell any lingering scent from the candles though. They must not have been lit in years.

He bent down and opened a cabinet taking out a pile of red towels. "There's soap, shampoo." He indicated the more feminine bottles by the tub.

Why did he have those? Were they from another girl or another witch his father had kidnapped? Had his father lived here until recently? A small house for the powerful Dark Angel.

"I'll leave clothes on the bed."

My gut clenched. Would he be waiting for me when I finished or walk in on me as I bathed?

"The bathroom door locks." He must've read my mind or expression. "I'll close my bedroom door and be in the kitchen."

"Um, thanks." I wasn't sure about this nice version of Onyx.

He left the bathroom and I locked the door. Of course, if he could use magic to make a wave carry me into his arms, he could unlock a simple door. Standing, I debated the best course of action. He was being nice and I was wet and stinky. I turned on the water, stripped off my clothes, and left them on the floor. I'd be quick. Getting in the tub, I wondered if I'd need to wash the clothes in here or if he had an actual washing machine. Or maybe he could magically clean them.

The calm water soothed my nerves. I wanted to stay and soak but I didn't trust Onyx completely. I washed myself and shampooed my hair, rinsing it out with the running faucet. Twisting off the water and opening the drain, I stood and grabbed a towel to dry myself. I wrapped the towel around my body and stepped out of the tub.

Hurrying to the door, I unlocked it and peeked out. The bedroom was empty and the exterior door was shut. I grabbed the clothes on the bed and went back to the bathroom, locking the door again.

Slipping on the black leather corset, I cringed. This was almost as bad as the banshee bikini top. The bottom came to a stop mid-abdomen and displayed my belly button. The upper part made of black lace came to a V where the leather hugged my breasts. I couldn't wear this outfit.

Picking up the bottoms, I noted the slim-fitting black pants were similar to the pants Onyx wore. The leather had metal zippers and cutouts where weapons or wands could be stored. The bottoms flared wider. I shoved my legs inside and examined the entire picture in the bathroom mirror. He had to have something else for me to wear.

Bending down, I took my sister's compact out of the wet jeans and slipped it in one of my new pockets. Even though the it was old and broken, it was the one piece of home I had. And Jinx had said it possessed magic.

I flipped it open and waved my fingers. Nothing. I whispered a simple spell. Nothing. My magic didn't work down here and I didn't know what magic the compact possessed. It must have power because Jinx had bragged about it.

Opening the door, I peeked into the bedroom again. It was empty. I snuck to the other door on the wall and opened it. A closet filled with more black clothes. I grabbed a leather jacket and slipped it on.

"What're you doing?" Onyx stood in the doorway.

"The top you gave me was a little small." At my response, he cocked an eyebrow. "And I was cold."

"Cold in purgatory?" Arching a disbelieving brow, he marched to the shelf and took down a book. "Quick bath. My mother would always be in there for at least an hour."

I shrugged. "I don't spend a lot of time getting ready." Truth. He didn't need to know the real reason I washed and dressed so fast. "You wouldn't happen to have any looser-fitting clothes?"

"No." A muscle ticked in his cheek. "I've got boots for you in the kitchen."

His gaze went to my toes and traveled slowly up my body. He was checking me out. Balmy prickles spread across my skin. I wasn't used to warlocks ogling me. The only one who'd ever really noticed me was Lukas.

I wanted to squirm but I refused to express my discomfort. "Stop looking at me."

"You're short." While he was really tall.

I had to tilt my head up to see into his eyes. Maybe he wouldn't want a short girl for his Red Queen. Not that I wanted the position. "I wasn't considered short in the coven." Especially now that I'd used the Get Big potion.

Silence greeted my declaration and he continued to stare. Tension quivered in the space between us, affecting every part of my body. My head spun. My bones softened. My skin trembled in expectation.

I shuffled my feet and glanced around the room again. "What's up the stairs?"

He swaggered toward the bed and patted the pillow. "If you stay with me tonight, I'll show you."

A shimmer of temptation ran through my blood but I tamped it down. I didn't even like Onyx. His only allure was because he saved my life and his kisses were hot. Kisses I supposedly needed to breathe. "No."

"Too bad." He strolled past me with a gleam in his dark eyes. Waving me out the door, he shot a secretive smile understanding that I was tempted. "I guess you'll never know."

I huffed and straightened my shoulders. I didn't need to know what was up there. Maybe it had something to do with his job as Dark Angel, maybe whatever was up there was how he knew about the deaths overnight.

Marching out the door, I decided what was up the intriguing staircase didn't matter. He didn't matter. I wouldn't be staying long.

He shut the bedroom door and locked it, keeping me from peeking.

Curiouser and curiouser.

CHAPTER NINE

The bright red teapot whistled and I startled.

Onyx and I had spent most of the morning in stilted conversation with me asking questions about his world and his life and him avoiding answers, and him asking me about my life.

He strutted toward the stove, flicked off the switch, and lifted the kettle. "Do you want a cup of tea?"

"Sure, thanks. You drink a lot of tea."

Drinking tea didn't fit his bad boy image and yet he'd already had three cups this morning.

"My mom told me tea is restorative for dark magic." He used a spoon to scoop loose tea leaves into a diffuser and placed it in the boiling water.

"You don't use magic to make tea?" I'd always flicked my wrist for whatever food or drink I wanted, or at least I used to before my several imprisonments.

"Mother said magic would reduce the effect of the tea." He took down two teacups from the shelf and poured the steaming liquid in, then he brought both cups to the table and took a seat.

He'd had a real connection with his mother. Years later he still listened to what she'd told him.

I sat in the chair across from him and took a sip. The scene was so domestic. I wouldn't have expected it from the Dark Angel. "Did you live here with your father?"

"No." Darkness crossed Onyx's expression and he rubbed the bridge of his nose. "It was just my mother and I until she died."

My heart squeezed for him and anger pumped through my veins. "Your father let you live here alone? You were so young."

A gleam of something flashed in his eyes. He relaxed back in his chair and shrugged. "Are you going to keep running away?"

He'd completely changed the subject and I wasn't sure I should answer his question. He didn't answer mine and I didn't want to alert him to my plans. Not that I had any specific plans. But I'd never stop running away from him. From this place. "Maybe."

He burst out in laughter. The deep rumble rolled through my chest and brought a surprised grin to my face.

"You don't think I can escape?"

"No one ever has." His slow confession sounded sad.

Had he tried to leave? Or had his mother tried? Was that how she'd died?

"My friends are amazing. They'll rescue me." I pushed confidence into my voice.

Leaning forward, he placed his elbows on the table and his chin in his hands. "Is one of those friends someone special to you?"

His terse question set off alarm bells. Was he angry or jealous? I didn't know how to respond. I didn't want to make him mad, but if I told him there was someone maybe he'd leave me alone. My heart weighed the decision. Although Lukas might be coupled with my sister now. Her taunt about werewolves mating for life kicked me in the gut.

"Maybe," I said again.

"You're wishy-washy." He pointed a long finger at me.

I giggled. "You sound like an old lady."

Standing, he pushed back the kitchen chair and it clattered to the ground. He stalked around the table in three large steps. My eyes widened and I tilted back. I'd angered him. He grabbed my hand and yanked me to a stand so forceful that I fell against his hard torso.

My chest hammered. What was he going to do?

"Would an old lady do this?" His mouth plundered mine.

My body stiffened at the instant assault. He couldn't just take what he wanted. I struggled against him and opened my mouth to bite his lips. He slipped his tongue inside before I could react. Loosening his hold on me, he caressed my neck with a fingertip and his mouth persuaded.

I could easily break away. I should break away, break off this kiss.

He loosened his hold more, almost as if asking permission.

My instincts took control and I couldn't help but respond. There was instant chemistry between us. Tingles exploded as fireworks through my blood. My body broiled and I pressed myself closer to him.

My hand reached up and I grabbed the back of his head. My fingers wove through his thick locks. With him, I couldn't control my urges. I'd never acted so aggressive. He put his hand on my lower back pressing me against him. I moaned.

Our tongues entwined in a dance as the kiss changed to softer and less challenging. My tingles morphed to spirals of curled warmth. My pulse skyrocketed. Enjoyment buzzed and traversed across my skin and through my body. I wanted his kiss and his closeness. I ran my hand down his back, sensing his strength.

He broke off the kiss and stepped away, staring at me with eyes hazed by desire.

I staggered back. I didn't understand how he had this effect on me. Was this kiss about passion or helping me breathe? I wasn't sure of the difference or if the Kiss of Afterlife was even real. Onyx said his father kissed his mother so she could breathe. Or was that something they'd told a small child?

I tilted my chin to a haughty angle. I couldn't let him know my thoughts or feelings. "Was that kiss so I can breathe or for *your* pleasure?"

"That kiss was just for you, babe." He jutted a hip and stepped close again. I inhaled his unique scent.

"Come on." I took a step back. "If this Kiss of Afterlife is real, how often do I have to endure it? For how long? I was able to sleep through the night without it."

"You took a big risk not sleeping with me." His lips twitched. "If you gagged in the middle of the night, I wouldn't have heard you."

"I don't believe you." The entire concept was preposterous.

He lifted a dark brow. "So you're experienced with kisses then?"

Heat rose on my cheeks and scorched with the lie. I scanned the ground. I wasn't about to admit out loud he was my first kiss.

"When I kiss you for real, there will be no doubts. And eventually, you'll fall in love and beg for my kisses."

His bold words slapped.

"As if." My numb brain couldn't come up with a better retort.

He dropped into his chair and sipped his tea as if nothing had happened between us. As if giving me my first, second, and third kisses wasn't a big deal.

I could do the same. Act like this entire discussion was of no emotional consequence. Sinking onto my seat, I went to pick up my tea and noticed my fingers were shaking. I clenched them in my lap.

The silence between us dragged. My brain whirled with thought after thought and question after question. One of the many things bothering me about last night wouldn't stay quiet. "If you never leave your house after midnight, how did you find me when I arrived?"

"I didn't say I never leave after midnight. I said you shouldn't." He shrugged again. "Cerb was agitated, kept pawing at the door. He knew you were out there."

The dog appeared beneath the table, jostling the legs with his large size. Onyx bent down to scratch him.

Startled, I didn't think I could ever get used to a three-headed dog appearing and disappearing, sometimes leaving only his three mouths showing. *To watch or guard me?*

Cerb lifted one of his heads to stare at me.

"Cerb barked this morning when I was in trouble too."

Onyx patted the dog's first, second, then third head. "There are a lot of bad things out on the banks of the River Styx. Keep that in mind next time you try to run away."

⟫⟫⟫⟫ ⟪⟪⟪⟪

Onyx wouldn't scare me. Well, not with his warnings. His kisses scared me enough to want to leave. And to stay. No, leave. I definitely wanted to leave.

Onyx had stormed into his bedroom and slammed the door after our discussion. He'd been in there for hours and I didn't know if he was sleeping, reading, or working. What exactly did he do? The Dark Angel was shrouded in mystery except for the scary stories I'd been told growing up.

The Dark Angel lived on the banks of the River Styx and guided the dead down the river. The last Dark Angel, Onyx's father, had been in his position for hundreds of years. He'd committed to a witch or warlock a long time ago and would rule until they died so they could go down the River Styx together.

Mistress Lita had fallen and Onyx had said she and his father had gone down the river together. Now, Onyx was the Dark Angel with the powers and duties that role encompassed.

A shiver ran through me. I hated how I was drawn to his darkness. How I wanted to lighten his outlook and his world. But I could only do those things by staying here, which I refused to do.

I gave Cerb a final scratch as he lay at my feet. "I'm going to take a walk."

Which wasn't an actual lie. I would be walking, or maybe running.

Cerb lifted his three heads. He didn't move from his position. I took it as a good sign. Slipping on the boots Onyx had given me, I wondered who they'd once belonged to. It didn't matter. I stood and tested them out. They fit, which was the only important factor.

With one backward glance, I left, surprised the dog didn't stop me. And surprised Onyx left me alone for so long. This imprisonment was different than the others.

This time when I slipped through the rocks, I checked the river level. The muddy water flowed swiftly but not across the banks. It didn't tumble or roll like ocean waves.

I relaxed and hiked, keeping my attention on the river. My feet sunk into the sand leaving a deep mark. The silty banks climbed steeply until they became molten rock. A volcano must've carved this entire area, or the heat from hell. The rocks jutted out with slippery surfaces and sharp edges. An accident waiting to happen. I kept to the sand.

Above, darkness cloyed. Would I ever see the sun again?

Large, clawed footprints imprinted in the sand. It resembled a crow's foot only ten times bigger. I peered up. The bird must be larger than a human. I shuddered and hugged myself. Maybe the birds are what shrieked at night.

Stopping, I surveyed the area. I needed to get back to the place where I'd fallen. It would be the best place for my friends to find me. Not tucked away in Onyx's house or falling into the river.

I marched on.

Another footprint showed in the sand. I bent closer. This wasn't a bird's or some creature's. This footprint was human—a skinny, barefooted human. My chest lightened. If it was human, there had to be someone else on the banks of the river.

The print was skeletal. So it wasn't Onyx's. His feet were big. My hope rose higher and I scanned the area.

There was another skeletal, human-like footprint and another.

I followed the prints. They wound up a sandy path and stopped. The ground felt mushy. I twirled around trying to find what direction the person had gone. They'd vanished.

Kind of like Cerb.

So strange. To be fair everything I'd encountered down here was strange and unusual.

I tapped my finger against my chin. What should I do next? I could continue in this direction but there was no hint of anything going this way. I could follow the footprints back to where they began and see if I could find a new path. I could continue searching for the spot where I'd landed.

A squelching noise caught my attention, followed by barking.

Thinking of the three-headed dog must've brought him out of the house.

My knees bent and my body wavered. I glanced at my feet. My eyes popped. My feet had vanished similar to the footprints.

No, not vanished. My feet were sinking into the ground. My gut tightened.

The sand had become spongy enough for me to sink. I tried to lift one foot and then the other. The mushy sand pulled and I couldn't lift them. I gasped. Frantically, I yanked my leg up. It didn't budge. The wet sand was holding me down. I tried to shift the other leg. My body sunk further into the ground.

This wasn't normal sand. This was quicksand.

My body stiffened and I couldn't think for a second. My mouth finally worked. "Help!" Although I didn't know who I yelled for or if anyone could hear.

I jerked and pulled and wiggled. I sank deeper. The quicksand covered my boots and came to my knees. The wet rough sand rubbed against my leg through my pants. It wrapped around my legs and compressed. It was going to strangle me.

Onyx hadn't warned about quicksand. He went out during the day all the time. And yet every time I left, I encountered life-threatening trouble.

"Onyx!" I screamed and wiggled.

The barks came louder.

"Cerb!"

I sunk to my waist. My breathing became quick and panicked. Would I die in this horrible way? I lifted my arms so they wouldn't get stuck in the quicksand too. I didn't know what to do. The more I moved, the more I sank. I inhaled slowly. I had to stay calm.

Cerb trotted up the path.

I didn't want him sinking with me. "No, Cerb. Stay." It's quicksand. I wished I could telepathically explain the situation. "Don't come closer."

There wasn't enough time to send him to find Onyx. I had to figure this out on my own.

"Can you find a large stick, Cerb?" I trembled, imagining sinking lower and lower until my face was covered. No Kiss of Afterlife would help me then. "Or a bone. Fetch a bone."

Cerb bounded away and I sunk a little deeper. My breath came in short and shallow pants. If I sunk much more, I'd suffocate. "Hurry, Cerb."

The dog ran back toward me with a big bone in its mouth. He stopped right where the ground became squashy.

"Okay, boy." I had to think fast. "Hand me the bone and hold on. Do you understand? Hold on."

Three heads nodded at me. He did understand. He bent low and stuck his middle head out. Using his tongue, he positioned the end of the bone between his teeth.

I stretched my arm out, trying to keep it above the quicksand. Flailing my hand, I missed the bone. My body and my heart sunk further. "I need you to get a little closer. Don't fall in."

He braced his hind legs and stretched his neck to reach further.

"Good boy." I extended out again, tilting forward and stretching my hands. Wrapping each of my fingers around the bone, I shifted further forward. My body tensed. This had to work. "Okay, Cerb. Now pull me out. Play tug of war with the bone. Don't let go."

Please don't let go.

Growling, he tugged on the bone, shaking one head back and forth while the other two scanned the area.

My body lifted and dragged through the sand. "It's working! Keep going boy."

Cerb growled again. He backed up his body and hauled the bone further. The sand puckered and sucked at my clothes and skin while the dog hauled me out. He kept steady pressure. Inch by inch, I lifted.

Hope grew with each tug. I swung my other arm and grabbed onto the bone with my other hand. "Almost there, Cerb. We can do it."

He gave a final yank and my body plopped. I lay on hard ground for a second and then scrambled away from the quicksand to collapse on the ground.

Cerb licked my cheek. His strength saved me.

"We did it! We did it." Pride straightened my spine and gave me energy. I jumped to my feet and shook off some of the slimy sand from my clothes and hair. Standing tall, I scratched Cerb under one of his chins.

The dog nudged my back with his head. He was ready to go home.

"You go home, boy." Onyx's house wasn't mine.

Cerb whined and stood his ground.

I put my arms around his middle, thick neck and kissed the top of his head. "Thank you. I'll be fine."

Would I? When I'd run out of the house early this morning, I'd been swept away by the river. This time, I almost died by quicksand. But I had to stay confident and stand on my own. Cerb had rescued me, but it had been my idea to use a bone. I couldn't count on Onyx and his dog to help me. I had to escape from the banks of the River Styx on my own.

"Go home to Onyx." I dropped my arms from around his neck. "Be a good boy and listen."

Cerb quirked his heads, considering my request. Pivoting, he paced away while one of his heads kept glowering back at me.

Loud squeaking came from above. A dark shadow flew over my head.

A cold quiver went down my spine. *What now?*

A fuzzy white bird with long spiked eyelashes came into view. Its mouth was outlined in black and set in a permanent smile. A creepy smile. A double set of white wings appeared velvety. It resembled a butterfly or a moth.

My gaze followed the bird while my pulse skittered.

The ghostly moth swooped down. Before I could scream, claws dug into my back. Agony slashed through me. My feet dangled off the ground as I was lifted. "Cerb!"

The huge creature carried me away.

My shoulders sagged, causing the physical and emotional pain to deepen.

My destiny was to never be the hero, only the damsel in distress.

Chapter Ten

My body flapped in the strong breeze and the moth carried me higher. Horror leached in my midsection. My lungs shrieked and yet I couldn't scream. I was too terrified.

Terrified and hopeless.

Each time I tried to leave, to rescue myself, I ended up in more danger.

The River Styx flowed far beneath my dangling feet. We flew so high, higher than I'd originally fallen, if that was possible. Could I reach up and access the Archeron Barrier, the blockade between the coven and the Underworld?

Cerb barked below.

There was nothing he could do to save me. He was a spec on the ground.

The flying creature followed the muddy river to the left. The thought of being dropped and eaten by the nasty ghoul fish in the water mashed in my brain.

Tensing, I kept repeating to myself. "Don't drop me. Don't drop me. Don't drop me."

The river curved and flowed as the water picked up speed. Peering into the distance, the area around the river grew darker and darker. Pitch black, unlike the dark gray of the rest of the area.

Where was this thing taking me? Was I going to be its dinner? How could I escape?

The air thickened and I felt lightheaded. Because of the atmosphere, my terror, or because I needed another Kiss of Afterlife from Onyx?

The cliffs rose around us. Crooks and crannies had been scraped out of the sides. Occasionally a tree would stick out of the hard ground, seeming alien. The entire place seemed like another planet. I was adrift in more ways than one.

A light flashed and I gaped. A cliff shaped into a point, similar to a tower in a castle. The tower rose from a building made of rock. I squeezed my eyes shut and opened them again. It definitely was a castle. Could it be the old Dark Angel's?

The castle was hidden by a large rock formation. From below, it would appear to be a cliff. From my current vantage point, I saw balconies and windows and lights. A strange plank or sidewalk stuck out of the tower.

My chest pounded to an upbeat rhythm. This could be my escape. Others were here. I'd seen footprints and now I saw lights in the windows. It wasn't just me and bullheaded Onyx.

Guards dressed in red patrolled the castle. They were thin, skeletal. Kind of like the footprint I'd found before sinking into the quicksand. I shivered, remembering the squelch of my body and the ickiness of the wet sand.

I needed to escape this place because I kept going from one disaster to the next.

Staring at the castle, I must be hallucinating. Onyx had told me he was the only one who lived here. My thoughts went dark. Had he lied? For sympathy or to guilt me into staying?

The moth creature circled around and around making me dizzy. I couldn't focus on the castle because I spotted strange lights. Beautiful colored shimmers of lightning coming through the darkness. Gaping, I took in the sight. It resembled the Northern Lights swirling and crackling and flashing.

This might be the Underworld but it certainly was a wonderland. An interesting, dark wonderland with mystic enchantments and weird creatures.

The moth gave off a high-pitched caw.

I stiffened, bringing my attention back to my real predicament. It didn't matter if there were others in the castle, I was currently in the clutches of an eerie creature. It probably wanted to eat me.

The moth swooped lower as it continued to circle. I wished it would travel by the strange lights or the hidden castle. Either would be preferable.

The moth plummeted.

And I plummeted with it. Oxygen rushed out of my lungs. "Ahhhhhh!"

A grove of trees rushed toward us. I didn't know which was worse, falling into the river or crashing into a tree. Foliage existing in this desolate land shocked me. They were so out of place, kind of like the castle.

The moth slowed and did a wide loop as if searching for something. I gobbled a breath. Each tree in the grove was humongous, as tall as some of the cliffs. The trees sprouted strange orange fruit in the shape of an eggplant. One fruit was four times the size of me.

I panted. If the moth creature had plenty to eat, it wouldn't want me for dinner.

Flapping its wings slower, the moth made the circles smaller and smaller as it zeroed in on one tree. The moth wove through black branches with thorns and hovered above one of the orange fruits. The overripe fruit had holes and black spots.

The moth's talons released and I fell.

Screeching, I raised my arms trying to grab onto something. Anything. My muscles flexed and contracted. I had no control.

I plopped into the rotting fruit in one of the smashed indents as if I was a pit in the middle of the fruit. With shaking fingers, I clung to the spongy substance. My entire body trembled. What would happen next?

Would I ever get back to my old world? My eyes stung, but I couldn't cry. Too much terror shredded through my veins banging and bulging, swelling and shrinking. It felt as if I were taking the potions again.

Sticky juice from the fruit covered me from head to toe. Was the juice a marinade before being eaten? Either way, I desperately needed another bath. I missed Onyx's little house. I even missed Onyx.

Checking my body with my hands, I found no rips or holes in the jacket and pants. The creature didn't hurt me. How was that possible? Its talons had dug into my back. This strange world was confusing and infuriating, including the animals and the one person I'd met.

Emotional pain pinched. Would Onyx even wonder what had happened to me?

The ghost-like moth cawed again and flew away.

My shoulders drooped. The creature wasn't going to kill me. At least not yet. Peering down, I froze. If I fell out of the fruit and off the tree from this height I'd die.

I had to sit and wait. I tried to get comfortable and not sink into the mushy fruit. My hands were sticky and my clothes clung to my body from the juice. I recognized this fruit. A bowl of it had been sitting in Onyx's kitchen. It must be safe to eat.

I licked my hand and the tangy flavor tickled my tongue. "At least I won't starve to death."

Reclining in the squishy fruit, I sipped on juice and enjoyed the strange lights for awhile. I had no clue how long I sat there. I could almost imagine I was on vacation. Except for the fact I was so high from the ground and could easily fall.

But this wasn't a holiday. It was a kidnapping. And oh my stars, I was tired of being kidnapped. When I got out of this and escaped from the Underworld, I was going to create a potion to prevent kidnapping.

The entertaining lights swirled and crackled in colors of green, purple, aqua, and blue. The hued brilliance must be coming from above, from earth and the Kingdom of Alandaska. Onyx had said the Archeron Barrier between worlds had closed. But had it? Had he lied about this too?

Cerb's bark echoed up the tree.

Bracing myself, I leaned over the edge. Cerb stood below with his front paws on the trunk of the tree. "Cerb!"

My tension eased. He was going to rescue me again. I loved the three-headed dog. Why had I ever been afraid of him?

"I'm up here." I waved my arms back and forth.

The dog jumped, scratching at the bark. But he couldn't climb the tree. I was stuck here. Not just because of the height but because my entire body was covered in sticky fruit juice.

A breeze zoomed past my head.

Quivering, I ducked thinking the moth creature had returned.

This was no moth.

My mouth dropped open.

Onyx flew above me—an avenging angel. Or a dark one.

His black wings spread out from bare shoulders. The wings appeared feathery and smooth, and highlighted his wavy hair and dark eyebrows. His bronze skin shined with the glow of magic. My heart sprinted. His bare torso rippled with six-pack abs and carved pecs. Plus, the magical tattoo. His legs were clothed in the same black leather pants that rode low on his hips. His feet were bare.

Heat rose on my skin and my pulse skyrocketed. He was beautiful.

Onyx sailed toward me with his arms out. He scooped me up, his strong arms under my legs and behind my back, and spooned me against him. A waif in distress, I collapsed against him. My savior.

I'd rescued myself from the quicksand and stepped right into another danger. I tried to escape on my own but maybe I needed help from friends. Or even a Dark Angel.

He glided down, cradling me as if he cared. I melted further into his arms. Closing my eyes, I appreciated the essence of Onyx.

Bad boy. Angel. Enigma.

Blowing out a slow breath, I shifted my body because I was plastered to his skin and I didn't want to get too close. I couldn't let him take charge just because he rescued me. "I'm getting you sticky."

"I can drop you." His arms loosened and I started to slip.

I clung back to him. "No." *Never.* I was glad I didn't say the last part out loud. Flying with him was completely different than flying with the moth. He held onto me gently.

"You have more than fruit juice on you." He scowled. "What is this sandy stuff?"

"Quicksand."

Before I could tell him what happened a shadow flew over us. A shadow enveloping my relieved spirit.

The ghost-like moth was back. It darted toward us.

"Watch out." I ducked closer to Onyx, knowing he'd protect me. If I stayed with him, he could safeguard me from anything evil. Except maybe himself.

"It's a vampire moth." He chuckled. "Harmless."

"Not harmless. It kidnapped me." Reliving the terror, I shuddered.

"It's okay." Onyx opened his hand. A ball of orange fire formed on his palm.

The moth circled around us again.

"The vampire moths were terrified of my father." He opened his hand again. This time the ball of orange fire grew bigger.

"Maybe they don't know you're the boss now." I was mad for him. He was the Dark Angel and everyone should respect him.

"Am I?" He tossed the fireball at the moth.

The creature flew away and I relaxed until I realized what he'd muttered.

My brow furrowed. "What do you mean, you're not the boss?"

"Nothing." He glided down and landed on the ground.

But he didn't take action to set me down. He wasn't even breathing heavily. Those muscles of his were real and I was getting way too comfortable in his arms.

"You can set me down." My peevishness scratched in my ears. *Be cool, Cassia.* I didn't want him to realize how his closeness affected me.

"I don't want to." His voice dropped into a sexy timbre. The deepness rumbled through my chest and settled in my soul. He angled closer to my lips.

My ribs constricted. Did he plan to kiss me again? Temptation tingled just out of reach. I wiggled in his arms. "Put me down."

Our gazes battled like our tongues had during an earlier kiss. He kept taking what he wanted without giving me a chance to say anything. "I said, put me down."

He swung my legs and slowly let me slide down his body to the ground. I sensed every bump and ridge of his body. Each touch was a caress. My skin heated and my heart raced.

Staggering back, I glanced away and peered at Cerb. "Thanks Cerb, for saving me." I pet him and one of his tongues lolled out and licked my hand.

"What about me?" Onyx placed his hands on his hips.

He wanted me to thank him too. The dog probably alerted him to the danger and he'd come to my rescue. But the words refused to come out of my mouth. He didn't need more praise. He was cocky enough.

Smirking, I held up my hands. "Fine. You can lick my hands too."

He grabbed my hand and jerked me against him once again. "I want to lick more than your hand."

My body blazed. How was I going to resist his sex appeal and charm?

Chapter Eleven

We both bathed after getting back to Onyx's home, and now we sat in the kitchen drinking tea. A habit I was going to continue when I got home, if I ever got home. He seemed to enjoy the ritual, while I enjoyed the comforting warmth.

He'd found me another outfit, similar to the first, with leather pants and boots. Except this time the soft, silk shirt was more conservative with a mock collar and short sleeves. He was beginning to understand my taste, and possibly my personality.

"So you think the vampire moth," I shivered remembering its creepy grin, "didn't mean to hurt me?"

"They're herbivores." He wrapped his long fingers around the delicate cup displaying the contradictions between him and his environment. "They use the fruit as a nest. That one was young and female. She might've thought you were her younger sibling."

I scrunched my face in horror. "I don't look anything like her." Did Onyx think I did? I smoothed my wet hair.

His damp strands curled at the ends and his face shined after a shave. He wore a slightly different pair of black leather pants and had thrown on a loose black T-shirt so I couldn't see the shape of his broad shoulders and carved abs. Or the spot where his wings came from. "Her larva are black and pale."

I visibly shuddered this time, overemphasizing the motion. "Can you find me clothes in a different color?"

He laughed at my joke and I smiled. "Do you prefer red?"

"No." I shook my head. "Red stands out too much."

And I didn't want my clothes to constantly remind him about asking me to be his Red Queen. I didn't want to stay down here and rule by his side.

"Too bad." He frowned in disappointment.

Cerb appeared under the table at my feet and I petted him. "He's such a sweetie. Why does he become invisible?"

"My father scared him when he was a pup." Onyx rubbed his crooked nose. "It was then that Cerb vanished for the first time. Then whenever my father was around, he'd disappear. I don't know if he can control the invisibility or not."

I scratched the dog harder. "Cerb scared me when we first met but I've grown to love him."

"He cares about you too." Onyx's dark brows drew together. He seemed concerned.

Concerned about what? He must not appreciate that I was becoming attached to his dog.

"I know." Reassuring thoughts ran through me. "Cerb has saved me and warned you when I was in trouble."

"You're always in trouble." Placing his elbows on the table, he stared.

"Not until recently." I had been the model daughter and student, always trying to be nicer and smarter and more obedient than my sister. It hadn't helped me with the family dynamics. Even in the human dungeon, I'd been a role model prisoner until I'd met Destiny. She'd become my hero and I'd become her foot soldier. Helping her with her plans to escape the dungeon and the banshees.

"So you're only a pain for me?" Onyx's lips twitched before his gaze narrowed and became more intense.

Swallowing, I wasn't sure how to respond. Ever since I decided to be the main character in my own life story, I'd gotten into trouble. I'd ended up here because I wanted to be a hero and save my sister. Twice I'd left this house and gotten into scrapes and this time he'd saved me.

I had made his life difficult. "I've made your life more interesting."

The deep timbre of his chuckle rolled inside me and I wanted to lean into his enjoyment, experience the ups and downs of the tone. Once his laughter settled, he continued to study me as if trying to peer inside my soul or figure out my future.

No one had ever really looked at me to see how deep I went. Maybe he didn't want a Red Queen who was always in trouble. Or maybe he no longer wanted me at all.

My shoulders dipped with dejection and I immediately rejected the emotion. It was good that he didn't want me. Maybe he'd help me leave.

Onyx was a hero. A dark hero.

And while I found it irritating because I had wanted to rescue myself and failed every time, I should accept my sidekick role and ask him to help. Me leaving would make his life less stressful.

Pushing his chair back, he stood. "What kind of animal do you have for your familiar?"

A simple question for most witches my age. I clutched the teacup handle, wondering about the abrupt change in topic. All witches had familiars by sixteen. Mine hadn't arrived. He might think less of me when I told him I didn't have one.

Maybe I should lie.

Avoiding glancing at him, I scratched the dog under each of his mouths. Playing along, showing him that I could be nice and we could have a civilized conversation might help my case when I make the big ask. "I don't have a familiar yet."

"Oh." Onyx grabbed his cup and wheeled toward the sink.

The atmosphere between us became strained and I didn't understand why. We'd been getting on so well since strolling back to the house when we were both sticky. We'd talked and joked, and when we got back he'd been a gentleman and let me bathe first. The new clothes were on the bed when I was done and I'd quickly slipped them on. The spiral staircase had tempted me but I knew he waited to use the bathroom and I didn't want to get caught.

As he bathed, I'd explored the rest of the house by opening every cabinet and drawer, hoping to find a clue about Onyx.

No, not a clue about him. A clue on how to leave.

He picked up my empty cup and put it in the sink.

Standing, I ambled to the couch and picked up a thick book sitting on the side table. "I appreciate your taste in books." The book was one of my favorites and it proved he was a deep thinker. "How do you get books down here?"

"My father had thousands in his home. I brought them here a few at a time." Onyx dropped onto the couch and put his feet up on the coffee table. "In his hundreds of years, he'd read every one of them."

I'd never thought about what the old Dark Angel did with his free time. I'd known him as a terrorist of witches. Onyx had inherited the role, but he didn't seem as bad. Not like the scary figment of my imagination that his father had been.

Onyx was just a sexy figment of my imagination.

I jolted. I couldn't think that way about him. "Where's your father's house? Why don't you live there?" My brow scrunched remembering the castle in the cliffs. Had it been real?

He studied his cuticles. "My father forced my mother out of his place and into this house. I chose to stay with her."

When he didn't say more, I prompted, "It's cozy."

"It reminds me of her." His lost tone caused my defenses to crumble.

I wanted to comfort him but also feared getting too close. I wasn't thinking of him as my enemy and I should. I needed to stay focused and strategic, pretend to be friendly when really I was digging for information.

Cerb must've sensed my empathetic sadness because he appeared at my feet and nuzzled his head against my knee. I rubbed his chin, making us both feel better. The dog should be comforting Onyx.

"Now that you're the Dark Angel, isn't your father's house yours?" The image of the castle in the cliff came to me again and I shivered. This house was more welcoming.

Onyx took his feet off the coffee table and stomped them on the floor. "His place is cold and huge. One guy roaming around there would be..."

"Lonely." I understood and related. I'd lived in a small house with three other people and I was still lonesome. I couldn't imagine living in a large empty place.

Scanning the living room and kitchen, I noted the simple and efficient design. It was cozy and comfortable, and you couldn't hear any of the strange noises from outside. If he'd just clean it up, the home would be a perfect place to live.

"Unless," His swift action had him sitting right next to me on the couch. "You become my Red Queen."

The spark of temptation surprised me and I shut it down. I'd hate being in eternal darkness. I'd hate having no friends. "No."

He took my hand and squeezed. Did he think he could persuade me with his touch? Maybe he could because sizzling quivers rolled through me. "We'd live in a huge, secure mansion. No fear of vampire moths or ghoul fish or...anything else."

The castle I'd seen must be what he was talking about. I was positive.

He drew my hand against his chest and I felt his heart beating. "Together, we'd be the gatekeepers of the Underworld."

"That's a position you can share?" My mind whirled searching my memory for what I knew about the Dark Angel and the gates to the Underworld. "Did your father and mother share the position before she died?"

"No." He flung my hand away and stood. "My father didn't share anything."

Gripping my chin, he tilted toward me and forced his mouth onto mine. He gave me a quick, hard kiss as if punishing himself for his father's cruelty. Even with its briefness, my lips tingled, yearning for more. Pivoting on his heel, Onyx stormed out of the room and into his bedroom. He acted like an injured animal. I didn't understand what had set him off but I realized he was hurt.

Our shared emotions and experiences jarred me. He hadn't had a happy childhood and neither had I. Another thing we had in common. Empathy for him and his situation contracted in my soul. I felt for him. Felt more than his sadness. Felt his loneliness and concern.

His mind and his body enticed. Every time we touched, and every Kiss of Afterlife pulled me deeper into his orbit. His charisma kept me close.

Was I falling for my captor?

⇶ ⇷

I spent a restless night on the couch. If Onyx was a real gentleman, he'd let me have his bed. Thinking of the black sheets warmed by his body, maybe it was better if I stayed in the living room. Until I left.

He emerged from his room the next morning, stretching his arms. He was fully dressed. "What's your escape plan for today?" Sighing, he assumed he'd need to rescue me again.

I blinked. Was one of his powers reading minds?

Chuckling, he strolled into the kitchen and put on the teapot. "I can read your expression. You're so open."

My gaze narrowed. He acted so confident, like if he wanted to escape he'd succeed. I wished I had the same assuredness. I was done with my lame attempts to leave. "I'm going to go to the spot where I dropped down. When my friends come, they'll search for me there."

"I'll take you after breakfast." He took out a pan and rummaged through the cabinets. "I wouldn't want you falling into the river or quicksand, or being scooped up again."

By the time I emerged from the bathroom, he had two plates of bacon and eggs on the table. My stomach growled. He was a great cook, but not a great housekeeper.

After eating, and him tossing the dishes into the sink, he grabbed his leather jacket. "Let's go. I've got something to do."

Onyx might want me to stay here, but he didn't insist. He didn't lock me up like so many others in my past. Maybe he'd decided I was a bigger headache than I was worth.

We headed out the door and walked in silence. An edgy and uncomfortable silence. Tension arced between us. An electrified tension. A tension thrilling and tugging, one that had me waiting for the next thrust.

"You believe in your friends." He spat the words finding the sentiment unbelievable.

"Don't you?" The words shot out and I wished I could bite them back. He didn't have any friends.

We followed a path by the river. The water was calm and quiet at this moment. The cliffs and boulders surrounding us resembled a gigantic cavern. The dark pall hung over us like my unthinking and hurtful question.

"I don't believe in anyone but myself." Certainty rang in his voice.

Because he'd had no one else to count on. His mother had died, and his father had ignored him at best or was abusive at worst. I glanced at his crooked nose, knowing the bend wasn't natural.

Distress churned in my gut. Whenever he talked about his father, he rubbed his nose. Cerb had started disappearing around Onyx's father as if the beast was afraid of the man. "How was growing up with your father as the Dark Angel?"

"Great." A muscle in Onyx's cheek ticked. He was lying.

"Everyone in the coven was terrified of him. He kept kidnapping witches." What had happened to those witches? Were they running around the banks somewhere or were they living at the castle in the cliffs? Maybe they made the shrieking noises at night.

"My father was looking for his daughter and then his granddaughter and then his great granddaughter." Onyx sounded defensive.

"Destiny must be his great granddaughter." I'd realized she was related pretty quickly in the cavern where I'd fallen through.

"My father kidnapped my mother and that turned out okay." Forced positivity edged his tone.

Did it?

"What did you do before...coming here?" He changed the subject, clearly not wanting to talk about the other witches or his father.

"I'd returned to the coven after..." I wasn't sure I wanted to talk about this subject either. My life had been bad, although not as bad as his. Sulfur stung my nose and my eyes watered.

"After?" He nudged me with his shoulder.

It was only fair that I told him a bit about me. "I was in the human palace dungeon, then kidnapped by banshees."

"They're the reason you have the tattoo on your forehead. Tell me what happened." His demand softened at the end showing his concern.

My insides went mushy. He cared about me at least a little.

"That's Destiny's story to tell." Her adventures were an entire novel—or novels—on their own, while my life had been boring until I'd met her.

"I can get rid of the tattoo if you want." His sincere offer had me picturing the mark on my forehead.

I'd hated the mark at first. Jinx had taunted that I'd have the tattoo for the rest of my life and no one would think I was attractive. The symbol hadn't bothered Lukas. "Do you hate the banshee mark that much?"

"Tattoos are cool." Shrugging, he studied my forehead as we walked. "It's up to you."

I appreciated how he let it be my choice. Quickly telling him about my adventures under the human palace and when I'd been captured by the banshees, I tried to keep my storytelling short and unemotional.

His fists clenched at his sides. "That's terrible." Sympathy and anger rolled into his voice and I wanted to confess everything.

"When I came back to the coven, my family kept me captive in the basement while my sister pretended to be me."

"She must've been jealous." He took hold of my hand and used his thumb to caress my skin.

The tingles helped soothe my internal pain.

"Ha." My sister was the exact opposite of me. She wasn't jealous. I'd always been jealous of her. "She was just trying to trick my friends."

"Your friends again." He dropped my hand.

We continued in silence for awhile. He seemed to be stewing about my friends. Maybe he was jealous of me having friends.

Again, I sympathized. I needed to leave, and yet I hated leaving him alone. I took his hand this time and squeezed. "I'm sorry you're here alone."

He squeezed my hand back. "After what you told me, I understand why you feel trapped."

His words settled in my center. I did feel trapped on the banks of the River Styx but I also had never felt so free to be myself. I'd shared a lot with

Onyx even though I'd just met him and I never talked about myself or my beliefs so much before.

"Here's where I found you." He opened his hand and let mine slip out.

He was letting me go. My heart cracked. Fate had introduced us, and was now splitting us apart. He'd led such a lonely life but I couldn't stay. And even though my family was evil, at least I had my friends.

"Yes." I recognized the slick wall that climbed forever.

"I should go." He paused and glanced my way. "I have...things to do." Staring at the ground, he veered away. "I'll send Cerb to keep you company."

"Spy on me, you mean." The terse accusation swooshed out. I wasn't really mad about the dog. Onyx didn't trust me and he was leaving without saying goodbye.

Onyx wheeled back with a furrowed brow. "What're you talking about?"

"During my other attempts to leave, Cerb followed me." I clung to the façade of my anger. "He was reporting back to you, I presume."

"No." Onyx shook his head in slow motion while his eyes widened coming to some kind of realization.

He didn't share his realization with me.

The accusation died with a swift kick of guilt. I was the one leaving and he'd be alone. "Never mind. I'll send Cerb home when I leave."

"You're not going anywhere." Tramping back to my side, Onyx wrapped his arm around my waist and pulled me in tight. "But in the meantime, to keep you breathing in this atmosphere, I should give you one more kiss."

Anticipation and dread threaded through me. I yearned for another kiss. A real kiss not a Kiss of Afterlife. My muscles tensed and my mouth opened, expectation holding me in its thrall.

He lowered his head and stopped. "Unless you think your friends will be here soon, in which case you won't need my kiss."

I didn't know what to say. I didn't know if my friends were coming now or days from now. Would I have to walk away and say goodbye to Onyx each morning and then return to his house before midnight each night? He didn't believe my friends were going to rescue me or that I could leave at all.

I gasped, already out of breath. I could admit to myself it wasn't because I couldn't breathe in the atmosphere. It was because I wanted his lips on mine. "Just kiss me."

His mouth lowered ever so slowly as if trying to decide. On contact, sparks of joy spread from my lips to my chest, even though the two body parts weren't attached. My skin quivered and I moved my mouth against his without thought.

I wanted this kiss.

Not to breathe but to live.

He teased my lips apart and his tongue entered my inner sanctum. My knees went weak and I pressed closer to his strong body.

I swirled my tongue with his and we made a more intimate connection. I wanted this kiss to last forever. And yet I knew it wouldn't because we couldn't even have a relationship.

His body jerked away and he took a step back.

Onyx smirked. "Told you, you'd beg for my kisses."

Chapter Twelve

As Onyx strutted away, my fists curled in frustration and unfulfilled craving. He had said I'd beg for his kisses. I hadn't begged. It was simply a request. I heaved a shaky breath. Where did he learn to kiss so enticingly when he'd always been alone? It must come naturally to him. Did it come naturally to me?

I turned my back on him as he left, glaring at the rock wall. Worrying about his kisses wouldn't do me any good. I was leaving when my friends arrived and he couldn't stop me no matter how wonderful his kisses.

A heaviness settled in my chest. What about Lukas? I'd barely given him a thought. Of course, I had bigger things to worry about than another non-relationship.

Glancing up, I studied above.

At the top of the darkness, continuous stone covered everything as far as I could see. Instead of the invisible dome above the kingdom, it was a dome of solid rock.

How would my friends get through? Destiny had come down to visit the old Dark Angel, surely she could find her way down again. Hope stirred the heaviness making me more unsettled. How long would I survive without Onyx's kisses? The breathing kind. And how could I keep kissing him knowing I was leaving? Doubt seeped into any hope I'd held.

Cerb appeared in front of me. I scratched his three heads while my doubt and hope intertwined like a braided rope. That's what I needed. A rope to climb out of here. Except there didn't seem to be a way through the Archeron Barrier.

The dog dropped a bone in front of me.

Cringing, I picked up the bone and tossed it for him. I threw the bone again and again, until I got tired.

"Not now, Cerb." I sank onto the hard ground, exhausted even though I'd done nothing but throw.

He dropped the bone in front of me again.

"Lay down, Cerb."

Listening to my command, the dog laid at my feet.

Petting his supple fur, I loved having him by my side. It was as if he could read my mind and my emotions. He'd be a loyal companion. A thought convulsed through me. Onyx had been upset when I'd told him I didn't have a familiar.

Cerb's body stiffened and he lifted his three heads. Panting, he stood in front of me in a protective stance. He cocked his heads and lifted all six of his ears.

Unease chilled my skin. "What's up, Cerb?"

The dog stood alert. His ears stayed cocked.

The unease heightened and my hair stood on end. I got to my feet.

Cerb nudged me with one of his noses. He wanted me to run. Why? Was someone coming? Could it be my friends? My spirits lifted.

"No, Cerb." I pushed him away.

Whimpering, he lowered his body into a crouch position in front of me. He wasn't leaving. The idea of Cerb being my familiar snuck into my mind again. Could it be possible? Maybe the reason I didn't have a familiar was because he was trapped in the Underworld and couldn't come to me. Not because I was deficient as a witch in some way.

I bent down to pet him. Could he leave with me?

A loud shriek pierced.

The same shrieking I'd heard when I'd left Onyx's house at night. Other-worldly shrieking.

I froze and my gaze darted around. It wasn't night. It was early morning. Or at least I thought it was early morning. It was hard to tell in perpetual darkness.

In the blink of an eye, half a dozen...things jumped out at me.

Ghoulish, ghostly figures.

My insides compressed with horror, each organ trying to shrink and hide. The shrieking weren't people, were they?

Their flat bodies resembled playing cards. Painted red, they had spindly legs and arms and their hands had long, knife nails. Their misshapen faces appeared similar to *The Scream* painting with vacant eyes and a gaping black mouth. The skeletal body parts were barely recognizable.

Cerb growled. He'd known something was going to happen. I should've listened to him.

The strange red flat creatures marched closer. The Red Flats.

What did they want? My fingers wrapped around Cerb's throwing bone. How dangerous were they?

"Stay back." I brandished the bone in front of me like a weapon and took a step. It hadn't worked the last time I'd done this. Of course, Cerb hadn't been a real danger. But I didn't know that then. "What do you want?"

The Red Flats shrieked higher. The keen screeches came at different high pitches from each of them. The sound tortured my ears and made me dizzy. Was that their power? They had no weapons. They couldn't hurt me unless they drove me mad with the screaming. Or scratched me to death with their talons.

Cerb growled, baring his teeth on three heads. He backed up to the spot where I stood. He wanted to protect me. But I didn't want him injured.

The shrieking coming from the Red Flats caused my head to throb and my body to weaken. Forcing my arms up, I clutched my ears. But my hands didn't stop the noise from sneaking through. I had to get away from the screeching.

Squeezing my eyes, I spoke to Cerb in my head. *Cerb, I'm going to jump on your back and cling. You have to run through these things and get away. We have to get back to the house. And Onyx.*

I hoped Cerb understood. Otherwise, I'd fall on him and pass out from the high-pitched shriek. And the Red Flats would win.

Pretending I was fainting so they wouldn't suspect anything, I wobbled and fell face first onto Cerb. My body hit his fur—a big, fluffy cushion. Too bad it wasn't comforting at the moment. I wrapped my arms around his waist and gripped his fur between my fingers. *Am I hurting you?*

No. I'm a tough cerberus.

I lost my grip. He'd answered. Slipping, I almost fell off the big dog. My pulse raced and I regripped him tight. He had understood and responded in my head. I'd learned at the academy that was how a witch communicated with their familiar. Could it be true? Could Cerb be my familiar?

Cerb squatted on his front paws and growled.

My body tensed and fear curled in my gut. If I didn't live through this, I wouldn't need a familiar.

The Red Flats shrieked longer and louder.

The anguish in my ears hammered through my head. The dizziness increased and I hoped I could hold myself on Cerb's back.

Jumping up on his back legs, Cerb charged toward the Red Flats like a horse rearing up. Starting to slide, I pressed against his back and clung tighter. Terror rocketed inside as the dog launched forward.

The Red Flats' sharp nails flicked out with a zing. The nails extended into claws. Their talons were their weapons.

Horror scraped through my body like their protracted nails would scrape into my skin if we were caught.

The closest Red Flat stretched its skeletal arm. It got so close that I saw blood on its fingertips.

Is that why the Red Flats were red?

My stomach roiled.

Their nails struck at me.

My ribs constricted. Between the constant shrieking making me dizzy, the sight of blood, and the closeness of their fingernails, I couldn't handle much more. My eyes flickered closed. I didn't want to see what happened.

No. I forced my eyelids open. I wouldn't die this way and I wouldn't let Cerb die.

Run, Cerb, run!

He must've heard the panic in my mental communication because he made a quick right and wove between two of the Red Flats. The blood-tipped nails came within an inch of my face.

I heard a scraping noise and fright tore through me. Had it gotten me?

Glancing at my shirt and leather pants, I saw the material wasn't ripped. The nail hadn't penetrated.

Onyx. If he knew about these creatures, why had he left me here alone? Did he want me to die or become so scared I'd never leave his side?

Cerb careened through the rest of the Red Flats, knocking them down like bowling pins. With each tackle my body swung back and forth trying to avoid their wicked fingernails. Cerb swiveled right and pivoted. Gritting my teeth, I held on. He ducked and swerved around the final group of Red Flats. I forced myself to breathe as he galloped toward home.

Good boy, Cerb. We've escaped. Let's get home.

Not answering, he kept running. His pace slowed. He must be getting tired.

We'd escaped using my plan. Comparable to the incident with the quicksand, but this time there'd be no gigantic moth swooping me into more danger. I looked up to be sure. Tired of one misadventure after the next, I vowed to force Onyx to tell me everything about his world.

Keep going. You can do it. I cheered on Cerb.

He panted heavily and his pace slowed even more. I must be heavier than expected.

The angry shrieking started again. Louder and closer than it should be. The Red Flats were following us.

Anxiety sprinted from my toes, up my legs, to my center. We were getting closer to the cliffs in front of Onyx's house. We had to get there before the Red Flats reached us.

Cerb tripped and stumbled. His trot became uneven and sluggish.

Are you okay? I patted him on his side. My hand encountered something sticky and damp. Worry threaded through my bloodstream. "Cerb?"

His legs collapsed and he tumbled to the ground taking me with him. I braced for impact but didn't feel pain, overcome by concern for Cerb.

"Cerb!" Lifting my hand, I spotted the blood. Not mine. Cerb's.

Alarm rang in my head. I scrambled to his side and stroked one of his necks. "Cerb. What happened? Did one of those things get you?"

All six of his eyes were closed. His tongues lolled out of his mouths. His short and shallow panting mimicked a freight train.

Fear for him ratcheted up. "They scratched you didn't they, boy?" I leaned over his large body and found the spot where I'd felt the blood.

A cut about the size of one of those thing's fingers streaked between his fur. It didn't seem that bad. Why had he passed out?

The horrifying shrieking grew louder.

The screaming thumped in my head again. "The Red Flats are getting closer. We have to get to safety." I pulled at his neck. He didn't budge. "Come on. A few more steps. Get up and let's get you home."

Cerb didn't twitch. He stayed on the ground.

Worry and guilt raced and ended at dread. It was my fault he was injured. He'd warned me with his growls and protective stance about approaching danger and I'd ignored him. I'd told him to run through the Red Flats.

"Let's go, Cerb. You can do it." I didn't want to leave him alone.

I tugged on him again and again with all my strength. I couldn't lift him or pull him. He was too big and too heavy.

The shrieking came closer. My lungs contracted and I puffed trying to calm myself. We'd be surrounded soon.

Glancing at the crack between the two boulders, I gauged how long it would take me to run to the house and get Onyx. I needed help and if I stayed here, both Cerb and I would die.

"I'm going to get Onyx. I'll be right back. I promise." I patted him a final time before dashing through the crack. "Onyx! Onyx!" I ran toward the house, opened the door, and yelled, "Help me!"

Onyx emerged from his bedroom wearing his usual attire of leather jeans and vest. His droll expression came alert. "What happened? Are you hurt?"

His concern touched me. Breathing hard, I bent at the waist. "Cerb. Injured."

"What did you do to him?" Accusation and anger slashed across Onyx's expression.

"I didn't do anything." Offended, I wasn't going to argue with him. My feelings weren't important right now. "It was the Red Flats."

"The red what?" He grabbed his jacket off the couch and shoved his arms in the sleeves.

"Those things shrieking at night."

The shrieks infiltrated the house.

I placed my hands over my ears and bent again.

He rushed toward the door. "Stay here."

"I thought they didn't come out during the day." Accusation threaded my voice. What else had he lied about?

"They never have before." He narrowed his gaze to study me as if I was at fault. "Where's Cerb?"

Cerb's injury was my fault. I dodged in front of Onyx. "This way."

"Stay here." His hand grabbed the neck of my jacket, jerking me to a stop. "I'll find him."

"I'm going. You'll need help."

Shaking his head, exasperation showed on his face. He let go of my jacket.

Together, we slipped through the crack in the boulders. The minute we did, the shrieks echoed around us. The Red Flats were getting closer.

Cerb laid listlessly on the ground. His torso jerked up and down. He wheezed from his three noses. His tongues stuck out so far all three of them draped on the ground. His paws didn't twitch.

My heart strangled and my throat went dry. He had to be okay.

Onyx dropped to his knees. He stroked the dog. "How you doing, boy?"

His quiet tone steeped in sadness. Running his fingers through the dog's fur, he exhibited how much he worried about the animal. Cerb was important to him. The dog was Onyx's only companion.

If the dog truly was my familiar what would happen? If Cerb came with me, would Onyx be alone? Could Cerb even exit the Underworld?

"It's a little scratch." My voice rose.

I'd gotten Cerb hurt and I might be stealing him from Onyx. Conflicting emotions crashed inside my stomach and head. I might finally have a familiar and he might die because of me. "I don't understand how one little scratch can take him down."

Skreeetcheeetcheetch! The noise pierced the small valley.

My body tensed. The Red Flats were coming.

"It's not just a scratch." Onyx sniffed and his gaze held a sorrowful gleam. "The fingernails of the undead or Red Flats as you call them," his tone went terse and rigid, "their nails have poison. Even a little can kill."

I froze. Tumultuous thoughts stabbed in my already pounding head. Why hadn't he told me this earlier?

Chapter Thirteen

We were going to lose Cerb.

Lose him before I knew for sure that he was my familiar. My midsection emptied and hollowed. Onyx would lose his pet and companion. The dog's death would leave a black hole in my heart.

The shrieking became raucous and higher. Closer.

Skreeetcheeetcheetch!

Torn between sadness and fear, I didn't know whether to run or cry.

Onyx jerked his head to listen. "Get inside the house." He made no move of his own.

He wanted me to run to safety while he stayed and put himself in danger. My lungs hitched with an unknown emotion. I'd never had a personal protector before and now I had two. I hadn't listened to Cerb and now he was dying. Worry punched. If I didn't obey Onyx, would he die too?

Stubbornness firmed in my center. I wanted to stay and help Cerb. I wanted to be part of the solution, not run and hide like a gutless ghost. "Not without you. Not without Cerb."

More shrieking.

I scrunched my shoulders trying to control the agony in my head. This wasn't fair. None of this was Cerb's fault. "You're the Dark Angel. There must be something you can do to help."

"If I had full magic—" Onyx clamped his mouth shut. His sour expression set with an obstinate edge.

"What." Not a question, a demand.

"Leave."

"I wish I could." Sniffing, I let the terror take control. My body quivered and I locked my knees to stay standing. I'd been afraid of everything since arriving.

The shrieks came louder and nearer. The marching of the Red Flats skeletal feet resounded in my pulse.

Onyx stood, took off his jacket, and gave me a glance. He blew out a breath, shook out his hands, and lifted his chin. His obstinacy changed to hard determination. With palms up, he stretched his arms displaying muscles in the short-sleeved T-shirt. Light flared from his palms. Yellow and orange flames ringed his hands. The flames grew into a controlled fire, extending out toward Cerb.

Panic thrust inside and I grabbed Onyx's arm. "Don't burn him."

The flames flickered and he jerked away. "This is how my magic looks."

I tilted back afraid of getting scorched, by his fingers and his gaze. His dark magic was different from witch and warlock magic.

Onyx had demonstrated his power when he'd saved me from the overflowing river. His magic had resembled fire then too. His firepower hadn't extinguished in the waves or burnt me. He wouldn't hurt Cerb.

Dark magic was stronger. It worked in the Underworld, while my magic did not. Dark magic stayed connected to your soul even after you sailed down the River Styx, while regular witch and warlock magic died with the person. Dark magic was powerful enough to deal with the evil Underworld creatures.

Creatures Onyx hadn't warned me about.

The loud shrieking scared me out of my fascination with Onyx. I meant, with his powers.

He focused again. The flames shot out from his palms toward Cerb. The fire wrapped around the dog in a whirling, fiery motion. Cerb didn't react so either there was no heat or he didn't feel it in his current condition.

Perspiration formed on Onyx's upper lip. His gaze stayed on the dog, ignoring the shrieking. The flames grew wider with flares of blue and red. Gold dust sprinkled inside the fire.

The flames rose lifting the three hundred pound dog a foot off the ground.

I took a step back. Onyx had powerful magic and yet strain showed on his face. How much longer could he hold up? I'd been taught the Dark Angel's powers were immense. Maybe that wasn't the case. Or was it because Onyx was different? He wasn't born a warlock and descended to become Dark Angel. He was a direct descendant of the old one, which you'd think would make him more powerful. There was no history explaining his existence. He was the first.

My brow furrowed and I tensed. I wished there was a way for me to help. Maybe if I'd agreed to become his Red Queen I'd have powers and be able to assist.

The fire swirled around and around and whooshed forward toward the crack between the cliffs taking Cerb along for the ride. The flames licked the cliff walls causing the rock to blacken.

How were Cerb and the flames going to fit?

The fire modified and decreased in width, narrowing and revolving so Cerb and the magic could fit through.

The perspiration on Onyx's face increased. His arms trembled with effort.

While his magic appeared amazing, lifting a dog—albeit a heavy one—shouldn't take much power. Look what he'd done with the waves when I'd been trapped. If my magic worked, I could snap my fingers and lift the dog with no problem.

He followed behind the flames, keeping his arms aloft and his concentration focused.

I brought up the rear while questions pummeled my brain. I knew not to ask now.

Glancing behind, I saw a flash of red. My chest jolted. The Red Flats were almost here. With their thin bodies, many of them could easily slip through the crack and reach the house.

Squeezing through the crack between the cliffs, I kept turning my head back and forth. Cerb was halfway to the door with Onyx closely following. He might have heard the Red Flats through his concentration but he didn't know how close they were.

The Red Flats stood in the open area where Cerb had laid minutes ago. Their thin, skeletal red bodies probably wavered with the slightest breeze. Too bad there was no wind. I didn't know if they could sense us or not. But at some point, they'd go through the crack and find the house. Anxiety crept across my skin in an invading army of goosebumps. Or invading Red Flat creatures.

We had a few feet left.

The flames grazed the edges of the door. Would he burn the house down? If so, we'd have nowhere to hide.

Cerb crossed the threshold with Onyx right behind. The flames brushed the floor and walls yet did no damage. As soon as he was inside, I dashed into the house, slammed the door shut, and locked it. I slouched against the door. Adrenaline leaked out of me in waves.

While straining, Onyx used care in lowering the twirling fire to the ground. Cerb, carried by the flames, landed gently. The fire extinguished and Onyx collapsed next to the dog on the floor. He stuck his fingers in the dog's fur.

My heart swelled. He loved the animal and saved him from additional attacks by the Red Flats. Now, we had to figure out how bad the poison was in Cerb's system.

The Red Flats banged on the door and I jerked. "They're here!"

"They can't get in." Onyx barely whispered. "House protected."

I shivered and hugged myself. "You told me the Red Flats didn't come out in the day either. Are you sure we're safe?"

"Yes." He stroked the dog, expending his remaining energy to express his love.

Cerb lay unconscious. Had he even been aware of being moved? His shallow panting was getting worse. We had to do something to save him.

I jerked into action. "Do you have any fiddle leaf?" Hurrying to the kitchen, I started opening drawers and cabinets. I'd seen some bandages and ointments in one of them.

"Cabinet on the far right. Why?" Onyx cuddled closer to the dog.

"It heals and withdraws poison." I swiveled toward him. "Or does your dark magic heal?"

"I. Don't. Know." Anger punctuated each word. He struggled to sit up "When my father went down the river, I received a surge of power. And now…"

"Now?" I held my breath waiting for him to respond.

When he didn't, I grabbed the tin of fiddle leaf from the cabinet and bustled back to Cerb. I'd do all I could to save him from his injury while Onyx thought about his answer. Sitting on the floor, I used a tea towel with soap and water to clean the wound. I pressed the fiddle leaf against the scratch.

Cerb, can you hear me? I asked in my head.

He didn't answer.

"What does the fiddle leaf do?" Onyx went more pale.

From worry or exhaustion? It was hard to tell. Anxiety hurtled and bumped inside me making me ill.

I'd let him get away with not talking about his powers for now. Cerb was more important. I held the fiddle leaf in place. "It draws out the poison."

Nails scratched against the window. My worry buzzed and crashed. The Red Flats were right outside, still shrieking, still out for blood.

"I'm never leaving the safety of this house again." Adding a chuckle at the end, I half joked because I still longed to go home.

Onyx stared at me. The intensity of his gaze and the tightness around his lips showed disbelief, and maybe a little hope. He wanted me to stay. He wanted me to be his Red Queen. It only took a moment for his expression to change. His lids lowered and darkened. His lips lifted into a stiff smile. "Right."

I pushed the thought aside and broke the intensity of his stare. "What are the Red Flats really called?"

"My mother called them the undead." He'd mentioned the name outside. Slowly standing, he used the couch to prop himself up.

"Why didn't you tell me about their existence? Was it because you wanted me to stay and were afraid those things would freak me out?"

"No. You have to believe me. I've never seen them before today. I've only heard their shrieking at night." He wavered into the kitchen and put the kettle on. "Tea?"

Nodding, I pressed another fiddle leaf on the dog, hoping to draw out more poison. While tending the wound, I watched Onyx lean against the kitchen counter. "Why are you so weak?"

He bent his elbow and flexed a large bicep. "Who are you calling weak?"

Frowning with concern, I wouldn't let him escape with a joke. "Is exhaustion normal for a Dark Angel after using powers?"

"I don't know." He spun away from me to grab cups from a cabinet. "I only became Dark Angel three days ago."

He avoided my question. His father, the previous Dark Angel, must've taught him something. Or he could've learned by watching the man. "How can you *not* know?"

"Stop with the personal questions." Onyx's rough voice told me I'd get no more answers about him and his dark magic. "Or I'll ask you a few questions you don't want to answer."

We were at a standstill, at least about him. "What are the Red Flats really called?" I repeated my question.

The teapot whistled and he made two cups of tea. "Whenever my mother told me stories—"

"Horror stories."

"She explained they were undead who couldn't or wouldn't travel down the River Styx to their final destiny. Undead the Dark Angel couldn't round up. She said there weren't very many of them."

"She was wrong. Or just terrible at counting." I quivered, thinking about their sharp nails and blood-colored bodies. "Why are they red?"

"I don't know, but a scratch from their nails is poisonous."

They shrieked from outside. Would they ever go away?

Lifting the leaf, I inspected Cerb's wound. "Why? How?"

"So many questions." Onyx lowered his head acting disappointed. Did he wish he would've asked more questions of his father? "All I know is that the undead have changed. They weren't red before and there weren't very many. I'd been warned they were dangerous. They'd been trained to stay away from me by my father. I was protected."

"Cerb isn't protected. Neither am I." Unease crept up my spine. I couldn't leave and yet I shouldn't stay. And what about Cerb. If I left, could he leave with me? The dog could be stuck here. He might not even fit into my world. "How many undead are there?"

"I don't know. They've multiplied." Onyx's brow furrowed. He was planning something.

I held in a slight gasp. A couple of days with him and I was already recognizing his expressions and tones. I'd never been able to do that with anyone else. Clearly, because my sister was still able to trick me.

The shrieks came again but they sounded further away. They hadn't scratched the windows or banged on the door in a while either.

"Are they leaving or just getting quiet?" A shudder went through me. I might be confined to this house until I figure a way out. "I thought you said I'd be safe."

"The undead have never come out during the day before." He glowered in a confused array.

"Why are they now?"

"Maybe it has something to do with your arrival." He shifted the blame to me, sending an arrow through my chest. "I was going to pick you up at dinner time."

He hadn't expected my friends to show up. Maybe they never would. Maybe they shouldn't because they could get hurt by the Red Flats too.

Onyx handed me the mug with steaming tea and I smiled my thanks. He was sweet and protective. He'd been planning to come get me for dinner. He wouldn't have left me out there alone at night.

He sat on the floor beside me and the dog. "Do you know if the fiddle leaf is working?

"Only time will tell."

❧ ➳➳ ☙

I pretended to read while Onyx sat with a book. Every few seconds he'd look at Cerb. The dog snored at our side. After a couple of hours, his breathing seemed more even. A good sign. My spirits lifted even though there was still a chance the poison ran deeper in his veins.

"He's a tough cerberus." I hoped what I said was true. I couldn't tell Onyx that the dog had told me himself.

"He is." Onyx set his book down. "Will he be okay if we left him alone for a few minutes?"

Nodding, I appreciated how he asked. When we'd first met, he would've simply told me what to do.

"Come with me." Standing, he held out his hand.

I glanced at the door. We hadn't heard any shrieking but I wasn't about to go outside.

"To my bedroom." His clarification brought new concerns.

My brows arched. "What? Why?"

"I want to show you something." He didn't say it in a seductive way so I guessed the thing he wanted to show me wasn't his body parts.

Ignoring the second of disappointment, I placed my hand in his and let him pull me to my feet. His fingers entwined with mine in a caress. Warmth slid along my skin and everything felt right with my world.

Except for the fact that everything was wrong.

I'd fallen onto the banks of the River Styx. I couldn't go home. I'd possibly met my familiar who was now injured and probably couldn't come home with me. And then there was Onyx.

Gorgeous, dark, and mysterious Onyx.

I didn't know what to do about him.

"Trust me." He tugged me into his bedroom and I let him.

I did trust him. At least to a point. I trusted him to keep me safe. Keep me safe from everyone but himself.

He walked right past the bed.

Relief and letdown whirled inside. I refused to acknowledge the latter.

Bracing his hand on the rail of the spiral staircase, he led me up.

My curiosity leapt. I'd been so tempted to climb up the wrought-iron steps and take a peek. I was glad I'd waited for him. Climbing the steps, I squeezed his hand tighter.

The top of the staircase led to a sliding glass door and balcony beyond. He slid the door open and we stepped outside. I gasped.

Beams of glowing illumination broke through the darkness above. Similar to spotlights or lightning swirling with colors of green, purple, aqua, and blue. Inside the colored beams, sparkling flecks of silver and gold fell—rain made of light. The luminous shafts held off the darkness reminded me of traveling through a witching glass or divine inspiration for art, music, and poetry. The lightning was far enough away that it wasn't dangerous.

Awe and revelation filled me with hope. I'd never expected something so incredible in a place so bleak. Lightness, reflecting the scene, whorled in my chest. "This is beautiful."

"There are a few beautiful sights down here, including you." He pushed back a strand of hair from my face. His intense gaze captured mine.

His expression was more glorious than the lights. The way he looked and treated me made me feel like a real queen. His gaze held me like how the lights held the gold and silver flecks. I wanted to sway toward him and let him hold me, let him be strong for me.

Startled by my thoughts, I broke his hold. "What are the lights?"

"My mother told me they were souls who had redeemed themselves and were now destined to become angels to guide living people. She called them Archeron Lights."

"Like the Barrier. The Archeron Barrier."

"I always believed it's where she went." His note of solemnness at the end broke my heart.

"Why do you think that?"

"She spent hours up here." He absentmindedly twirled my hair in his fingers. "I don't know if she felt closer to her home or if she was searching for a way to leave."

"What else do you remember about her?" I asked because he seemed to enjoy talking about his mother and I appreciated getting to know him better. He was finally opening up.

"She was beautiful, in a sad way. I don't remember her ever smiling." His expression soothed any tension. "She missed her home like you. She never expected to stay here forever. At least, at first." He cleared his throat and a muscle ticked in his cheek. "She told me she came to love it down here."

Was he trying to convince me or himself? Squeezing his hand, I could see the benefits. No coven manipulations. No competitions to see who was the most powerful witch. No annoying sisters. "Did your mother love the Dark Angel?"

"That's why she stayed." Onyx jerked his head down in a faux nod. He let go of my hand and my hair and faced forward, gripping the railing of the balcony.

I missed his touch. Shaking my head, I leaned against the railing too and watched the lights. Most likely his mother didn't have a choice except to stay. Onyx had told me I had no choice either when I first arrived. I wondered...

The lights glimmered brighter and flared.

I wouldn't ask or accuse at this vulnerable moment. I needed him to keep talking. "She stayed because of you."

"Maybe." He chuckled.

His laughter warmed me more than the lights. "Did you love the Dark Angel?"

"He was my father." Onyx sounded defensive.

I didn't want to upset him. I wanted to get to know him. "I love my parents. But that doesn't mean I like them." I'd already told him parts of my history.

"I'm sorry." He draped his arm over my shoulders in contentment and sympathy.

I wanted it to mean more.

We stood there in comfortable silence, watching the lights flash and zigzag and swirl.

My body relaxed and I leaned into him. This is how life would be if I stayed. We'd live here with Cerb. Even if he was my familiar, he could continue to be Onyx's pet. We'd read and discuss books and drink tea. He was a great kisser who appreciated me, unlike my family.

We'd be a perfect couple.

My insides jarred and I stiffened. I was falling for my captor. I was believing my current cage was gilded. And I was romanticizing my current predicament.

But I couldn't trap myself in a dark version of wonderland.

Chapter Fourteen

I dislodged the wonderland possibility from my mind and would contemplate the idea later. If Onyx was talking, I should be asking questions that might answer how to get home.

Shifting toward him, I let his arm slip from around my shoulders. "When we were outside with Cerb, you said something about your powers. Something about *if you had full magic,* and then you stopped talking."

His expression darkened and his mouth flatlined. "It's nothing."

"It must be something." Putting sympathy in my voice, I stroked his arm. A rush of sprinkles shot across my skin.

He pinched the bottom of my shirt between his fingers and tugged me closer. "I don't know how to explain."

He didn't want to explain. He was using his closeness to distract me and trying to act tough. Admitting he had a weakness would be difficult for him. I had to draw it out. "Try."

Tugging me closer, I waited for him to respond. Or kiss me. It had been a while since my last Kiss of Afterlife. Mentally, I put my foot down. I wanted to talk, not kiss. "I told you about how my parents treated me. It was embarrassing but I shared my inadequacies."

"You don't have any inadequacies." The conviction of his words had me angling closer.

Maybe I did want a real kiss.

He rubbed the cloth of my shirt again. "Take this outfit."

He wanted to talk about clothes?

"I snapped my fingers and your first two outfits appeared exactly how I wanted them."

Revealing—both the clothes for me and the admittance by him. "So you made me this sexy goth style."

Red spots appeared on his cheeks and he ducked his head. "As I got to know you, I altered the second outfit to be...a bit...more modest. After you were taken by the vampire moth, I went to make you another outfit and..." He dropped my shirt and his shoulders sagged. "I couldn't."

Leaning back from his confession, I tried to keep the surprise from showing. I rubbed his arm again, wanting to lighten the atmosphere. "So, you're not a fashion designer."

He didn't laugh. "I'm getting weaker." He placed his arms on the railing and leaned, peering down, seeming dejected. "Which makes no sense."

Worry and confusion wriggled. Was it getting worse with each use of his power? If he became weaker, he couldn't protect me. He couldn't get me home. I stomped on my selfishness. I couldn't think about myself. He might be my opposition, but I didn't want him powerless and in pain. I understood the feeling since I had no magic here. I placed my hand on his back and rubbed, letting him feel my sympathy and understanding. "You managed to get Cerb into the house."

"Barely, and it was a strain." He kicked at the railing with his booted foot several times. "When my father died, I experienced a jolt of electricity. New powers snapped and electrified in my blood." He lifted his head. Raw torment flickered in his gaze. "Now the power wanes as if it's being drained."

Another thing I could relate to. Both the dungeon and the banshees locked my powers and my sister stole my identity. "How long have you felt this way?"

He continued to stare at me causing foreboding to trickle through me. "Right after you arrived."

His words plowed, almost knocking me down. Shock, anxiety, and fear sliced into my skin, opening myself to internal wounds.

I held up my hands. "I'm not doing anything. I don't have any powers." I snapped my fingers and nothing happened.

Straightening, he took hold of each of my arms. "I don't know how else to explain."

I swallowed. I might already be stealing Cerb because I believed he was my familiar. How could I also be stealing his powers? I certainly wasn't gaining any. "Can you still fly?"

A teasing grin lighted his face. He let go of my arms and flew up. Waving, he flipped like a ninja fighter.

Amazed, I watched his graceful figure and my skin warmed. His movements were tight and tough, elegant and precise, limber and strong.

He flew back down and landed on his feet behind me. He pressed the front of his body against my back. Electricity charged. Maybe I was draining his power through this combustion between us.

I licked my lips. "Amazing."

He spun me around so my front pressed to his. "You're amazing."

His lips plunged onto mine and I responded immediately, opening my mouth and tangling my tongue with his. Whenever he touched or kissed me, I couldn't control myself. I wrapped my arms around his neck and dug my fingers into his thick hair, reveling in the silkiness.

I pressed against him and my skin tingled and sparked. He set me off in ways I'd never imagined.

His tongue swirled around my mouth, capturing me in an intimate dance. Breathless, I didn't understand if this was the Kiss of Afterlife or just a kiss. A real kiss.

He tugged on my hair and ran the flat of his palm across my back. His fingers caressed lower. I pressed myself even closer, yearning for more. My body ached for his touch everywhere.

A shriek interrupted our kiss.

My body stiffened and I perked my ears. "I hate those things."

Hated them and hated that they ended our kiss.

"They can't hurt you here." He wrapped his arms around me again and pulled me close, and I wanted to stay this way forever. "Because the undead have gotten so loud at night, I went searching for them after I left you this morning."

My lungs compressed knowing what danger he'd been in. I punched him. He was looking for trouble. "Are you mad? Maybe that's why they attacked during the day."

His lips lifted in a slow, cocky, self-assured smile. "Maybe I am mad. Crazy even. My mother might've been. It's why my father moved her out of his castle and to this house."

I softened with compassion until each of his words hit me. "Did you say castle? I saw a castle when the vampire moth carried me away."

He shook his head. "The castle is impossible to find. It's behind rock walls and built high on a cliff."

My brow furrowed. "Do you know where it is?"

"Of course, I do." He angled his chin in a superior manner. "The castle is mine now, but it's empty."

"Really?" My chin dropped. "Because when I flew over it there were lights on."

His body froze. He scanned my face. "I've got to go." He pivoted away.

My head spun and I grabbed his arm. I didn't want him dashing off without a plan. "Go where?"

He glared at me and the hold I had on his arm. "None of your business."

Hurt, I dropped his arm. I thought we'd opened up to each other. "We were talking." And kissing.

"And now we're done." He stormed off the balcony and took the spiral steps several at a time.

My chest twinged as I moved to the sliding glass door. I thought he cared about me. But if he did, he wouldn't abruptly stop this conversation and run off with no explanation. "I have other things I want to discuss."

"Like what?" Impatience lined his tone. He landed on the bedroom floor and scowled up at me.

I sagged against the top of the spiral staircase and peered down. "Do you really believe I'm the one draining your powers?"

"Who else?" He flung his hand. "You're the only thing different down here. You're the one who doesn't belong."

The word *belong* stabbed me in the back. The pain spread through my shoulders and arms and into my soul. He *did* blame me. "If you think losing your powers is my fault, then help me go home."

I didn't know what was happening with the coven or my friends. Who was in charge of the coven? Destiny, a warlock, someone else entirely? If Destiny wasn't supervising, what had happened to her and Stone? Was Lukas with my sister? He hadn't been present in the Subterrane Abyss cavern.

Was Jinx still pretending to be me? And what about my other friends? Helartha, Pith, Gnit, and Trolgar. What had happened to Violet? Last I knew, she was in a frozen-sleeping state and being held captive at the coven. What was going on in the Kingdom of Alandaska with the new king? And the threats from my sister?

So many things I needed updates on. I needed to know what was happening in the real world.

"You just want to go home to your special someone." Onyx spat the accusation.

Was he jealous of Lukas? It didn't matter. How Onyx and I felt about each other didn't matter. "Is that why you're running away? I want answers."

"So do I. Which is why I need to go." The roughness of his voice should've made me shut up. "Take care of Cerb while I'm gone."

"Wait." I stomped down the staircase one step at a time. He couldn't kiss me and leave. Although it wouldn't be the first time. "Where are you going? What are you planning to do?"

Was it dangerous, especially after recently draining himself?

"Dark Angel business and none of yours."

"What I want matters." I poked him in the chest. I might've spoken indecisively earlier, but not anymore. I didn't care about his Dark Angel plans and I wasn't waiting for a rescue. "I need to go back. I *want* to go back. Don't try to stop me."

"I won't." He grabbed my finger and flung it away. "In fact, I'm going to help you." He sounded just as determined. "Stay here and take care of Cerb."

I staggered back. "What? Why? I thought you wanted me to be your Red Queen."

Watching his expression, I searched for a hint of lying or subterfuge. How well did I know Onyx after all?

"You don't want to be my Red Queen. You want to go home. You've made that clear." A scratch in his tone hinted at hurt except that couldn't be possible. "If you're the one draining my powers, I want you gone too. I'm willing to make the sacrifice."

Sacrifice me and whatever relationship we might have had. Agony radiated in my chest and surrounded my heart. Onyx wasn't going to fight for me to stay or ask me again to be his Red Queen. He wanted me gone.

I wasn't as important as his powers.

Chapter Fifteen

I changed the fiddle leaf on Cerb's wound for the fifth time. When I reached out with my mind to ask how he was, he finally responded, *Better.*

My body wilted with relief. It was only one word but at least it was something. I'd become attached to him and if he was my familiar...then what? Could he leave the Underworld and come with me? And what about Onyx?

He didn't want me to stay. Which was good because I definitely didn't want to stay either. Right?

Onyx made me feel special. It might've started off rough, but I knew he respected me and my opinions which made me more confident. He cared about me and my safety. Is that why he wanted to help me find a way home? He wanted what I wanted? It was so unlike him. When we'd first met, it was his way or else. Had he softened?

Or was he lying and pretending to want to help? He'd demanded I stay and become his queen. He'd run out of the house without telling me anything. I shuddered, wondering where he'd gone and if he was okay. Worry for him chilled to the bone. The tough Onyx was the one I was attracted to but it was the sweet and compromising guy I'd kind of fallen for. Which one was real?

He would stay here and be the Dark Angel. I would return to the coven and warn the new king about my sister and Mistress Lita's evil scheme to take control of the kingdom. But with Mistress Lita dead and my sister unable to achieve the goal on her own, why did the kingdom need me?

Governing the coven didn't concern me. I only needed to find out about my friends and family. My eyes prickled. What would my parents and sister do when I came back? I wouldn't be stupid and naïve enough to become locked up again. But I still wanted to go home. I didn't belong here and now Onyx didn't want me to stay. My heart cracked a little.

Did he believe I truly was stealing his powers?

I picked up the book Onyx had been reading and settled on the couch, trying to avoid my confused thoughts and emotions. Hopefully the book would keep my mind off where he went and what he was doing. I'd take care of Cerb as requested. When Onyx returned, I had questions. Lots and lots of questions on how exactly he'd help get me home.

The front door opening woke me.

I jerked upright and the book I'd fallen asleep hugging slipped off the couch.

"I'm home, honey." Onyx's joking tone spiked my anger.

He had no right to joke when I'd been worried. He said he'd help me go home and yet he kept me in the dark.

"Where did you go? What did you find?" Standing, I picked up the book and threw it at him. "I was worried."

"I was careful." He dove out of the way and raised his hands.

His pleading action didn't lessen my anger. Or should I say worry. "Those Red Flats are deadly."

"I'm deadlier." He flashed his sexy grin—the one he'd used when we first met. The fake smile. "I'm the Dark Angel."

My frown deepened. He was acting again. I wanted him to be real with me, not some tough guy. His brag about being the Dark Angel struck remembering what he'd admitted about his powers being drained. I crossed my arms and jutted my hip, wanting to shake his confidence. "Are you?"

Onyx's expression grew dark. He strutted into the room and bent down to pet the dog. His expression mellowed. "How's Cerb doing?"

I wouldn't lie or refuse to say. Onyx worried about his pet. "Better."

"How do you know? He hasn't moved." The accusing glare had me sucking in.

Did Onyx know about my relationship with his dog? I didn't want to hurt him more by telling him Cerb *was* my familiar.

Saying it definitely in my head settled and felt right. Cerb *was* my familiar.

I couldn't take a three-headed dog home with me though. He might not survive in my world. Onyx never needed to know. "I can just tell Cerb's doing better."

Straightening, Onyx went into the kitchen and put on the kettle. He took out two mugs and flakes of tea, assuming I'd drink with him.

I was itching to know what he'd learned on his venture, but I didn't want to give him the satisfaction of asking because he'd been a jerk. So had I, and my nerves wouldn't let me stay quiet. "Did you see any of the undead?"

"No." He focused on me, blaming me. "I found evidence of where they're coming from."

"You didn't know where they came from before?" What he thought of me at the moment didn't matter. I needed to learn everything.

"I'd never encountered them during the day before so I never looked." He handed me a cup.

"Where?" I took a seat at the small table.

"They've taken control of my castle." He slammed the teacup down on the table and paced away. "And I'm going to take it back."

My pulse pounded and dread filled my veins like cement. Those things were deadly. "You can't fight dozens of undead on your own. Not with the way your powers are acting."

"I won't be on my own." Smirking, his gaze challenged. "You'll be with me."

I staggered back. "No. I'm not going near those things."

"I'll protect you." His confidence scraped a raw nerve.

Did he think there was nothing he couldn't do? I understood he was the Dark Angel but those things had chased us into the house. And his magic wasn't as powerful as it should be.

"You're protected against them." That was the reason he had no fear. His mother or father had cast a spell so the Red Flats wouldn't attack. "I'm not protected."

"Remember those lights I showed you?" He picked up his teacup and leaned against the counter, sipping his tea as if this was a casual conversation.

How could I forget? And why the change in subject? "Yes."

"The jagged beams of light actually revolve around the castle."

Remembering the beauty from his balcony, I thought about where the lights were located compared to his house. "That's not very far away."

He nodded. "The castle now has a bridge high in the sky. It goes out and retracts resembling a drawbridge."

"Why?" Why would someone build a bridge to nowhere?

"My question exactly. It wasn't there before. It's new."

"The Red Flats built a bridge?" The situation was getting stranger and stranger.

He swung his hand in a flourish. "I think it's a bridge to the beams of light. The light comes from above and when the Archeron Barrier thins people can go through."

People, meaning me. I squealed inside.

Then, I frowned and furrowed my forehead. "The Red Flats are trying to escape the Underworld." My realization charred down my throat with fear. "They'll terrorize the kingdom."

"I don't know…" Onyx tapped his finger on his chin. "The Red Flats aren't smart enough to build a bridge or know how to use it."

"Then who?" My fear zagged in another direction. "Warlocks and witches?"

"Normally, only warlocks can come through the Archeron Barrier to meet with the Dark Angel and he—now me—decides when, where, and for how long. If any random witch and warlock fall, like through a portal or a witching glass—"

"That's how it felt when I came through. Although my fall wasn't normal, it was because of a complicated spell." I jumped from the chair and spoke quickly with enthusiasm.

"And if nothing else works, I can fly you from the bridge and up to the lights." Taking a seat at the table, he stretched out his legs and crossed them at the ankles in a relaxed pose.

He had it figured out.

I didn't care that he acted like a jerk earlier. I ran to him, wrapped my arms around him, and hugged. He was going to help me get home. The breadth of his shoulders stiffened. The piercing pain of rejection made my arms as heavy as lead. He'd kissed me plenty of times, but now he didn't want a hug? I couldn't figure him out. He was tough on the outside, and yet he'd exposed his vulnerable side to me. I guess now that he wanted to get rid of me there'd be no more intimate conversations or real kisses.

My heart plunged. Awkward. I removed my arms, straightened, and took a step back. "Why do you suddenly want to help me leave?"

"Well…" He brought his legs in and took a sip of tea. He seemed to be contemplating if he should tell me the truth. "Maybe…"

"I thought *maybe* was wishy-washy." He was my captor but I teased him like a friend. I could admit I was attracted to his dark and sullen attitude. I appreciated the way he treated his dog and protected me from everyone but himself. I was intrigued.

He twisted his lips in a grimace. "Possibly...my mom didn't love it here as much as I stated."

His admittance to lying cut into my earlier thoughts about him being a friend. "You said she loved it here and loved your father."

What was the truth?

"Love might've been too strong of a word." He glowered into his teacup while his expression changed from grimacing to bland. "In front of him she pretended she was in love. When she thought she was alone, she cried and raged."

Remembering the broken furniture in this house, fear for him slashed through my midsection. "Did she injure you?"

I pictured Onyx as a little boy being emotionally and physically hurt by his parents.

"No." He rubbed his crooked nose. "She loved me. She told me so before she died."

I swallowed. "Did you see her die?"

"No." He stared into his cup with a blank expression. "She gave me a huge hug at night, said she loved me and she'd see me again. The next day she was gone."

He must mean that she'd gone down the River Styx and when he passed someday in the future, they'd be reunited. He'd lost his mother at the tender age of twelve and recently lost his father.

"I'm sorry." Remembering his recent rejection of me, I still leaned in and gave him a hug.

Onyx acted stalwart but he needed comfort and love. My heart jolted. I was only going to give him one of those two things—comfort. Because I was going home.

⟫⟫⟫ ⟪⟪⟪

"Here is where we'll approach the castle." Onyx used his finger to point at the schematic he'd drawn in the air using his power. The lines of the castle lit up in red and orange.

"Why don't we go at night, under the cover of darkness?" I wanted to sneak in and get out.

"The undead are most active at night. I'm hoping the other day was an anomaly." He spoke with confidence but there was a niggle in his voice hinting at doubt. "And here is a side entrance leading to the kitchen."

"How do you know this?" My nerves roiled. He hadn't been gone long enough to scout the entire castle.

"I lived there as a small child, and even after I moved here, I'd go to take Dark Angel lessons from my father." He used a cool tone as if his past didn't affect him.

His father had let him live alone in this house as a teenager. He was an evil Dark Angel. I hoped Onyx would make a better one and didn't start kidnapping witches to find his Red Queen. Since I wasn't going to be the one. My veins pumped green envy through my bloodstream. Nerves for the plan changed into anxiety for him. "Did your father ever say anything about possibly having your power drained?"

It had taken him a lot of effort to draw the schematic and it was already fading. We needed to plan faster.

"No." His expression hardened. He didn't want to talk about his powers. "I'm hoping I'll find answers in the library. Which is here." He pointed to a large room in the layout.

So in addition to helping me go home and retaking his castle, he had other motives for this risky venture. "Where will the Red Undead be?"

I combined our two names for the creatures and he nodded.

"Most likely they'd gather here," he pointed to a large throne room, "or here." He pointed to a dining room. The castle was huge.

"How do we find our way to the bridge?" My most important question.

"We go up. There are stairs here, here, here, and here. The castle gets narrower at the top."

The broad base of the castle transitioned higher and narrower, ending with a single tall tower. Half the foundation had been built into the cliffs. A narrow, walled bridge led up from the River Styx.

"We'll leave first thing in the morning, heading out to the east." He'd become General Onyx.

"That way leads to quicksand." My pulse fluttered. I didn't want to end up at the bottom of a dark, sandy pit.

"Good point." He might be the general of our operation but at least he listened to suggestions.

My nerves settled a bit. We were a team using each of our resources and knowledge.

"We need two final things. Weapons and clothing."

Smashing my lips together, I hated to remind him how his powers were wonky and he couldn't tire himself out before we left on our mission tomorrow. "Don't waste your energy making clothes."

"Not just any old clothes. Protective clothes." He hurried into the bedroom and came out holding up large pants, a shirt, and a vest. All made of stiff, heavy leather.

"Wow! You're going to look hot in that outfit." I exaggerated a wink. "And by hot, I mean sweaty."

"No, you're going to look hot in this outfit." He winked back. "And by hot, I mean sexy."

"Those clothes aren't going to fit me. They're huge." I giggled. "We're they made for you?"

"Yes, they're my clothes." He held out a black leather belt. "You can use this belt at the waist. Try them on."

"I don't know." I could tell they'd be huge on me with or without a belt.

"Go."

I took the clothes and went into the bedroom. After putting them on and cinching the belt around my waist, I gazed in the mirror. The black leather pants went past my ankles and dragged on the ground. The sleeves of the maroon leather shirt flapped at my hands. The black vest cinched in at my waist and pressed my breasts down.

Wearing his clothes felt too intimate. I'd have to show him how ridiculous I looked. I strutted out the bedroom door as if I was on a catwalk, something I'd seen my sister do in front of warlocks dozens of times.

"What do you think?" I twirled around.

"It will do the job." His intense gaze roamed over me and steamed me from the inside.

Shifting on my feet, I was uncomfortable with the visual caress. I'd be leaving and he'd find a new Red Queen. "I'll be lucky if I don't trip on the pants and fall on my face."

He bent down and rolled up each pant leg. "These clothes are made of armored leather. The claws of the Red Undead can't penetrate."

I appreciated how he used my combination of words for those terrible things.

When he finished rolling the pants to an acceptable length, he trailed his fingers up my legs and over my hips. "The hips have extra padding so if you fall or are knocked on your butt, you won't scratch your skin."

Every graze from his fingers zinged up my spine.

He cinched the belt tighter and I warmed in my center. "Obviously, the belt will keep the pants on. Too bad."

I shook my head, unsure if he'd even spoken the last two words. Was he hinting at something more? My mouth opened and I snapped it shut. I couldn't speak, couldn't ask.

Rolling the sleeves, he stroked my skin beneath. Definitely on purpose.

Balmy shivers tingled my skin. My pulse picked up pace.

He trailed his fingers up my arms to my shoulders and kept them there. "The shoulder pads are thicker for protection."

I held my breath. Where would he touch next?

He skidded his fingers across my collar bone in a slow, seductive brush. "The shirt and vest will protect your chest."

Not my heart. The organ pounded with every contact. I didn't know where I wanted him to touch next, but I knew I wanted him to continue.

Tugging on the collar, he pulled the shirt high on my neck. "You want to cover as much skin as possible."

Did I? At the moment, I wanted to take everything off.

Progressing up my body, his gaze caressed my face. Our lips were inches apart and I longed for a kiss. I licked my lips, then stopped my tongue from moving.

No, no, no. I couldn't get involved with him any longer. Kissing would only be used for when I needed to breathe. Speaking of which, when was the last time he'd given me the Kiss of Afterlife? It might be time now. "If I'm going to be wearing your protective clothes, what will you be wearing?"

His eyes lit with a gleam. "Nothing."

I imagined him naked and grinned. "You're going into battle naked?"

Because that's what this was, a battle. With the Red Undead. And between us.

The left side of his mouth lifted in a semi-smile, knowing where my thoughts had gone. "I'll be wearing regular, normal clothes."

"Your regular clothes don't have the protective features of these." I tried to keep my mind on the important topic. It kept being swayed by my desires. I wanted to kiss him but I was too scared to take what I wanted.

"I want you to be protected. You're more important."

His concern played me like an instrument. I was swept away by his caring. Pushing my fear aside, I wrapped one arm around his waist and the other around his neck. I forced him closer and pressed my mouth to his. It was the first time I'd initiated a kiss with him.

With anyone.

It was the first time I'd wanted to. He was giving up his protective gear to protect me. He was helping me go home.

Gratitude and parting soon gave an urgency to the kiss. In a way, this was goodbye.

I forced the seam of his mouth open and teased with my tongue. In and out and in and out.

He moaned. No rejection or stiffening of his body. He melted into me.

It was the first time I'd had control, *taken* control. Power thrummed through my veins, but not the magical kind.

He yearned for me. And I longed to give him what he wanted.

My hand reached under his shirt and brushed his muscular back. My fingers set on fire. His wings came from back here. Curious, I stretched a little higher, kneading and fondling a little more aggressively while trying to distract him from my goal.

I trailed kisses along his neck and blew in his ear. My fingers inched higher.

"Hold on." He dug his fingers into my arms. "If tomorrow goes as planned, we'll be going our separate ways. Never see each other again."

"I know." Which is why I wanted to kiss him, be with him tonight.

Pushing me away, he heaved. "I can't do this."

"But—"

"No." He strode toward his bedroom and slammed the door shut. The lock clicked.

He'd barred me from his bedroom. From his arms. From his kisses.

CHAPTER SIXTEEN

The next morning, we gathered the supplies we needed. I packed fiddle leaves and bandages in a small bag. Onyx revved a circular saw. When he'd trudged out of the bedroom, I couldn't look him in the eye.

Last night, I'd initiated a kiss and he'd rejected me. Similar to the one time I'd hugged him. His reasons for not kissing were the exact same as my reasons for kissing.

We'd be parting ways soon. Hopefully.

My heart bruised. Unbelievable that I'd miss him.

"What's the saw for? Are you planning to cut trees?" I chortled at my own joke. More so because I was nervous than actually funny.

"It's a fully-charged bone saw." He shoved the tool into his large backpack and a knife in his belt.

I shivered, not wanting to think about why he even owned the tool. Reaching down to pet Cerb, I tripped on my long pants.

"How ya doing, boy?" I bent down to scratch one of his heads and my chest contracted. Would this be goodbye?

"Ready?" Onyx wore his usual attire of black leather pants, T-shirt, and vest. I knew the clothing didn't have the special protective armor.

Was I ready? No.

My immediate internal response blazed down my throat. If our plan worked, I'd be going home and never see Cerb or Onyx again. Instead of voicing the negative, I nodded and stood. I couldn't display my sadness because Onyx didn't know of my connection with the dog.

Cerb got to his feet. He was almost back to normal. The wound was healing and most of the poison had been drawn out of his system.

"Be a good boy, Cerb." Onyx patted each of the dog's heads. "I'll be home soon."

My gut tightened. He hadn't said *we'd* be home. I scanned the living room and kitchen of the small house one last time. I'd miss this place and the owner. Still, I wanted to go home. I had to go home. Pulling back my shoulders, I scuffled toward the door carrying my bag where I'd hidden some of Onyx's tea leaves to keep as a souvenir.

Cerb padded toward the door.

"I said, stay." Onyx signaled the command with his hand.

Cerb quirked his head and three sets of eyes stared at me. *You're leaving?*

Air evacuated my lungs. *I need to go home.*

What about me?

I glanced at Onyx, then back at the dog. *This is your home.*

I want to go with you. Cerb whimpered out loud at the end. *I should be with you.*

You need to stay and keep Onyx company. He'd led such a lonely life. I couldn't take away his pet, even if I never got another familiar.

"What's going on?" Onyx stepped between me and the dog. "Are you two talking?"

I froze and shifted my feet, not knowing what to say. "Not really talking...more like communicating."

Distress flashed on his expression. He placed his hand on the dog's back possessively.

Holding up my hands, I tried to placate. "I think...because Cerb saved me...we've grown a bond or something."

Onyx's gaze narrowed and his brows furrowed. He didn't believe me. "Well, tell Cerb to stay put. He's been poisoned once and I don't want anything to happen to him. He needs to stay where it's safe."

I will protect you. Both of you. Cerb pushed a nose against me and a nose against Onyx. The animal cared about both of us. It would be hard for him to leave Onyx too. No, *I* wouldn't have a hard time. We'd just met. The idea that Onyx and I had formed a connection was preposterous.

"Cerb is insisting he can protect me—us." Tripping over my tongue and my feet wasn't a good start to our dangerous plan.

I didn't know how to tell Onyx the three-headed dog was my familiar, especially knowing I'd be leaving without him. I'd be breaking both their hearts. And mine. Although I wasn't sure if Onyx's heart was involved where I was concerned. But between the sweet and passionate kisses, and giving me his protective clothes, I knew he cared at least a little.

"Cerb, stay. That is an order." Onyx's terseness showed his adamance. "Cassia, let's go."

My eyes stung as I pet Cerb one last time. "Will he listen?"

The dog stayed standing.

"He always listens to me." Onyx raised a dark brow and angled his head. "At least he did before you arrived."

Another thing I'd changed since arriving. Cerb didn't obey Onyx. The Red Undead were now coming out during the day. Onyx's powers were being drained. My lungs hollowed. All things I might've caused, bringing more danger.

It was best that I left. And left alone.

We headed out, slipping through the cracks of the boulders guarding his home and following the path on the banks of the river.

Onyx took my hand and we walked in comfortable silence. His strong presence gave me confidence. I had to remember this feeling when I was gone and use it to build my own confidence in the coven. I'd be a different witch when I returned.

Stronger. Independent. Alone.

I forced myself to focus on the passing scenery. We went around the area with the quicksand and kept a steady climb upward. The castle was at the highest point, between a cliff and the river. Scratches etched in the ground and I didn't know if it was from a strange animal or the Red Undead.

My body tensed sensing another presence. We weren't alone. *Cerb?*

Maybe.

I sputtered and covered it with a cough. The dog had listened to mine and Onyx's conversations and referenced our private joke. Cerb was intelligent and belonged to both Onyx and me. How would that be possible with Onyx staying here and me returning to the coven?

"You okay?" Onyx studied me.

"Yes. I'm fine." I swung our arms nervously while trying to distract him. Should I say Cerb had followed us? The dog had a mind of his own.

We hit a well-worn path held up by rocks and boulders placed below. If I tugged out a tiny pebble, would the entire path fall? Even in the darkness, the cliff holding the castle cast a long shadow. The sulfur scent burned in my nose. Onyx's heat kept me warm and cozy.

"It's nice being...alone." Did his pause hint that he knew Cerb followed us?

I choked on another laugh. I didn't want to snitch on Cerb, but if Onyx already knew maybe I should say something. Of course, he could tell me he knew the dog was here. "Yes, but it would be nicer if we weren't on a dangerous mission and I wasn't about to leave. I hope."

"You will." Onyx squeezed my hand, his confident happiness stirring my anger.

My feet pounded on the ground and with each step steam rose higher in my veins. He wanted me gone. He thought I was draining his powers. He'd asked me to be his Red Queen because there was no one else to ask. He'd stopped our kiss last night. Miffed, I tried to control the hurt spreading through me. But before we got too close and needed to be quiet, I had to speak my mind. I had to know his true feelings.

I yanked my hand out of his and stopped, unable to *not* exhibit my emotional pain. "I bet you can't wait to be rid of me."

"What? No." His evident surprise had him stumbling to a stop.

"You think I'm draining your power. You think I'm the reason the Red Undead are coming out during the day." The list of my faults raced through my brain, bumping around and creating a hammering headache. "You believe it's my fault Cerb got injured."

"Yes. I mean no." Yanking off the backpack and letting it drop to the ground, Onyx reached for me.

Despite all those things, he'd also helped me and saved me and shown me the beautiful lights. He was helping me go home. Indecision swayed the steam and acid in my stomach. I took a step back.

We stood on a flat plateau. Rocks circled us and the path diverged in different directions.

Tapping my foot, I waited for him to decide. "Well, which is it?"

Cerb growled.

"That *is* Cerb." Onyx's jaw dropped. "Did you know he was here?"

My midsection clenched. I should've told him the dog had followed us. "Yes."

"Cerb, show yourself." The tone Onyx used would've made me do the exact opposite and disappear. He threw up his hands. "That dog doesn't listen to me anymore. Tell him to show himself."

Worry tensed in my muscles. I didn't want the dog to get in trouble. "He's only trying to protect us."

"Protect *you* when he's *my* dog." Onyx's emphatic delivery didn't match his distressed expression. "Or is he even my dog anymore?"

I leaned back, fearful that he knew the truth. "Wh-what?"

Cerb growled again, this time it seemed to be directed at Onyx.

"I've been watching the two of you. Cerb knew the night you arrived. He's known every time you've been in trouble. Now, the two of you are communicating." Onyx pointed an accusing finger. "Cerb is your familiar."

My stomach swirled and whirled scorching up my throat. I looked up and down and up again. I didn't know what to say. I didn't want to lie but I also didn't want to hurt Onyx.

"You stole my dog." His voice rose higher with a mixture of anger and anguish.

"Don't worry. I can't take Cerb home with me." I'd miss both the dog and the guy. At least they'd be together.

"Are you sure?" Onyx's slow delivery hinted at his doubt. "You come here. Steal my dog and my h—"

Skreeetcheeetcheetch!

My pulse jolted and my gaze went as wide as possible taking in the terrible sight.

The Red Undead.

My body stiffened and my belly cramped. Flight syndrome kicked in, but I had nowhere to run.

Over a dozen of them surrounded us. Their sharp talons out and ready to kill.

Internally, I shrieked like the Red Undead. It didn't matter who Cerb belonged to. All three of us were going to be murdered.

Chapter Seventeen

"Cassia, run!" Onyx stepped in front of me taking a defensive stance.

My heart bumped and clamored for him. He was protecting me again. Meanwhile I'd accused him, questioned him, and lied to him about Cerb. Onyx and I had been distracted and the Red Undead had snuck up on us.

Skreeetcheeetcheetch!

I covered my ears and cringed, remembering how their screams made me weak and dizzy.

"Run!" He slipped the knife from his belt and held it up.

His demand cut through my covered ears and brain. The last time I hadn't listened, Cerb got injured. Panic had my body reacting in flight. I ducked under the Red Undeads' spindly arms and darted.

With each step conflict warred inside of me. Those creatures couldn't hurt Onyx because he was supposedly protected. But the rules were changing. It was early morning and they were out and about, stampeding and attacking.

As he'd stated, everything had changed since I arrived. His power, Cerb's obedience, the killing creatures' habits. Maybe the protection spell his mother had put on him was gone too. Or maybe his mother had lied.

My foot slipped on the rocky ground. I paused and took a breath.

The Red Undead slashed at Onyx. He dodged and swung the knife. There were twelve of them attacking him and more emerged around us. His protection wasn't working or was draining away parallel to his magic. He could be poisoned or killed. He wasn't wearing protective clothing. *I was.* I couldn't leave him on his own to fight.

But I didn't know his plan. I might get in the way.

I grimaced knowing that's what had gotten me in trouble last time I'd waited for a signal to slip into a fight. If I'd made it known I was in the cave with Destiny, she would've let me help her and I wouldn't have fallen to purgatory.

And I never would've met Onyx. My chest thudded.

Onyx ducked and sidestepped poisonous fingernails. I inhaled sharply. He pivoted and shoved his foot into the Red Undead's backside. I covered my mouth, trying not to scream. The creature fell to the ground.

I inched forward, watching as Onyx swung his knife in an arc. He took out two more Red Undeads. He threw a ball of his power toward a group of them marching forward. They demonstrated no fear. The colorful ball of light hit them and they fell like a house of cards going down.

He fought valiantly, but there were too many against Onyx and his reduced powers. I stretched on my toes as anxiety curled in my gut.

Cerb? Are you here? I reached out to him with my mind.

Of course. He reappeared by my side. *I won't leave you.*

Thinking and analyzing, I gripped his fur. *We need to help Onyx or he's going to lose this battle.*

A Red Undead lengthened its arm and his talons shot out. I winced. With less than an inch, Onyx wheeled around. The nails missed him by millimeters. I let out a long breath. He tossed another fireball and the flat creature went up in flames.

My pulse ticked like a countdown clock.

This is what we're going to do. Quickly, I told Cerb my plan. It had to work.

My nerves fluttered. Cerb couldn't get poisoned again because it would react faster the second time. A basic potions and poisons lesson. But I also had to save Onyx. I wouldn't back down. I had to fight.

Cerb disappeared and trotted away from the backpack which still lay on the ground between the battle and the spot where I stood. I wanted him to be as far from the action as possible. I stared at the spot I'd told him to go and waited. My pulse throbbed, ticking off the seconds.

He reappeared further away, at a distance from the backpack and myself, and howled.

In time with his signal, I dropped to the ground and crawled toward the backpack. Wheezing, I felt as if I'd run a marathon. But I understood it wasn't exhaustion, it was adrenaline.

Several Red Undeads swung their claws toward the howling.

Onyx cut one down with his knife.

One more gone.

Cerb disappeared. He reappeared a few steps further away.

All the oxygen evacuated my lungs. The Red Undead who weren't focused on Cerb returned to fight against Onyx.

But I'd successfully drawn several away. There were still too many.

Reaching the backpack, I stayed low to the ground, scrunching my shoulders to stay small and unnoticeable. I unzipped the bag and took out the tool I'd laughed at when Onyx had shoved it inside. I couldn't imagine why we would need a bone saw. Now, I understood.

The skeletal frames of the Red Undead were bones dripping with their own blood. They were flat and thin and could be sliced off at the knees.

The bone saw was the perfect weapon.

Cerb disappeared again and stayed gone this time. I'd told him to run to safety. I hoped he listened.

The four Red Undeads that chased the dog reeled back toward Onyx. I positioned myself so they'd have to go past me first.

Mentally, I rubbed my hands together. Physically, I turned on the saw and stuck it out in front of the first Red Undead as it approached. My arms trembled. I couldn't show my terror.

The blade cut through the spindly legs like paper.

No sound. No scream of pain.

The Red Undead crumpled to the ground.

I thought I'd be grossed out at literally cutting them off at the legs. I wasn't. These things weren't alive, they weren't human. And they were trying to kill Onyx.

I slashed the next one's legs and it fell. And the next. And the next.

They obviously weren't intelligent. They must've had orders programmed in their heads and didn't know when to turn back or stop.

After taking down four, I crawled closer to Onyx. He fought more than a dozen. The Red Undead multiplied.

"Watch out!" He yelled and swung his knife so close to my head I thought I might lose it.

My heart stopped beating and I flattened myself to the ground. Letting go of the saw, I covered my head. My heart revved and restarted at a fast pace, pounding against the ground and echoing in my chest. I could've been killed by Onyx.

"Get up." He jerked on my arm, helping me get to my feet.

I picked up the saw I'd dropped. Onyx and I stood back to back. He held the knife and I held the saw.

"Quick thinking using the saw." He turned his head and flashed me a quick smirk. "Smart."

"Much smarter than you dropping the backpack because you were mad." Grinning, I couldn't believe I could tease at a time like this. Did stress do that to a person?

"We were discussing—"

"Arguing."

"Fine, we were arguing. And we'll kiss and make up later." He brandished the knife and slashed one of the Red Undead down.

My ribs constricted. Now he wanted to kiss? I crouched and used the saw to cut another one off at the knees.

"You laughed at the saw." He kept his back pressed to mine while we turned in a circle together. "You're not laughing now."

I sliced and took down another one. "I'm the bone saw hero."

"You're definitely something." His voice held a tinge of amazement and mockery.

"Now, it's your turn to be the hero."

He guffawed, hinting that he believed he was already a hero.

I wasn't going to give him the satisfaction of agreeing. "Use your dark magic to burn them."

"That takes a lot of power." His quiet voice admitted his weakness.

I couldn't believe he was that fragile. He could do something, pull out some sort of magic. "What about blowing them down. They're as thin as playing cards." My suggestion was greeted by silence and the whack of his weapon.

I used my saw to take another one down.

"My magic...my magic...

I knew what he was going to say. "Try," I urged him. "I'll protect you."

His body tightened with tension. He shifted his shoulders and tucked his knife into his belt. He stuck his palms out.

My own muscles contracted. He'd be vulnerable while accessing his powers. I had to protect him. Or we'd both die.

I swung the spinning blade back and forth, whizzing louder so they'd back off. They didn't. Wheeling around him, I kept the Red Undead at bay. If they came close, I took them out.

Onyx stood steady, pointing his palms at the path where the Red Undead kept emerging. Yellow and orange flames ringed his hands. The flames circled and revolved creating a slight breeze.

A breeze that wasn't even strong enough to blow my hair. And definitely not strong enough to take out the Red Undead.

My shoulders dipped. He was getting weaker. If this didn't work, we were goners.

Strain showed on his face as he narrowed his gaze. The fire shot out from his palms. The flames went around me and headed for our enemy. The fire flared with colors of orange, red, and blue. Sprinkles of gold twirled in the wind. The breeze picked up similar to right before a strong storm. My hair whipped. The paper-thin enemy wavered.

A final blast of air struck. The Red Undead toppled like a house of cards.

A smile burst on my face and success exploded in my lungs. Onyx had done it. He'd taken out the enemy. "You did it."

"We did it." He dropped his arms and staggered.

My center clutched. "Were you struck?"

"No." His pale face told me he was unsteady. The magic had taken a lot out of him.

I wrapped my arms around him. Half in a hug and half helping him to stay standing. Anxiety scorched unlike his magical fire. "Sit down."

He sank to the hard ground and held his head in his hands. "You were amazing."

"I know." I tried to keep my tone untroubled even as concern for him sank in my gut. "You were amazing, too."

"I don't feel so amazing." He swiped at his perspiring brow.

"We have to figure out what's happening to your magic." And if it was me causing the damage, I had to find a way to go home or not be so close to him. My heart ached.

Marching reached my ears.

"More coming." I gripped the bone saw and stood in front of him. This time I'd be the one fighting.

As if they'd multiplied, hundreds of Red Undead emerged from the original spot, from the other side of the path, and from behind us. Hundreds and hundreds of red bodies flashed as far as I could see.

My eyes widened. There were too many to count. My pulse spiraled around and around through my bloodstream. I didn't need the screams to become dizzy. My mind was circling in on itself.

We were surrounded by an entire army. An army of undead.

My ribs crushed and I spluttered. I glanced at Onyx, powerless and weak, lying on the ground. We didn't have a chance.

He staggered to his feet and I grabbed his hand, determined we'd both stay standing. After all we'd been through, we were going to die anyhow.

The Red Undead raised their claws on cue.

"Halt! I want to see who tried to invade." A high-pitched woman's tone tortured my ears. Almost as shrill as the Red Undeads' shrieks.

I huffed. Invade was a strong term for what we'd attempted.

"No one sneaks into my castle." Her fury arced to the point of rage.

"It's my castle." Onyx took a step forward while I held him up.

I didn't want him rushing into a bigger mistake. Maybe we could reason with this woman.

The army of undead separated in the middle. The owner of the voice strolled through the path, unafraid of their claws and poison. A strange crown of bones propelled forward. And so did the smell of death.

I barfed a little in my mouth.

A woman emerged from between the Red Undead with a regal posture. She was short and wore a red dress made of lace and heavy taffeta. Fur lined the collar. The skirt puffed out in a ballgown style, while the tight top displayed heavy cleavage. What looked like a human heart hung around her neck in a clear orb and was filled with something red and pumping. Her heavily made-up face attempted to hide her deep wrinkles and dark spots. The crown made of bones covered red hair, too bright to be real. She held a gold scepter with a large ruby on top.

Creepier than the Red Undeads. I shuddered.

Her black soulless eyes studied us. "Onyx, darling."

His face paled and his hand slipped from my grasp. "Mother?"

CHAPTER EIGHTEEN

M *other?*

Dread thudded. His mother was dead. Had he lied? By his shocked expression, he was just as surprised.

She strolled closer to us and I stiffened. This woman controlled the Red Undeads.

"I was going to get in touch with you. Soon." Her black eyes flared with magic. She gave him an air kiss by his cheek.

My family might not be demonstrative, but she hadn't seen him in years. She didn't hug him or even shake his hand. I was offended and grief-stricken for him. Why had she pretended to be dead?

She smirked in a cruel way, reminding me of Onyx's smile when we'd first met. Her lips barely shifted up and the harsh lines around the edges proved she smiled infrequently. "And who is this?" She spoke as though I was beneath her.

I scrunched my shoulders and my stomach clenched. I could tell by her expression she didn't approve of me.

Onyx cleared his throat. "She's—"

"Doesn't matter." Her cry went keen.

His mother was one of the kidnapped witches. She shouldn't have magic down here. Like me. And yet her eyes had flamed with power similar to Onyx.

What kind of power?

She rubbed the necklace hanging around her neck. "Arrest her."

"Mother, no." Onyx's urgent tone had me sucking in oxygen. He put his arm around my shoulders. "This is Cassia. She's...she's...she's with me."

Not a ringing endorsement. I held out my hand. "It's nice to—"

"She has a weapon." His mother's gaze narrowed. "She killed several of my guards. Murderer!"

I froze and glanced at my left hand. I still held the bone saw. I dropped the weapon and it clattered to the ground. Holding up both my quivering hands, I wanted her to know I meant no harm.

"Cassia's not a murderer." Onyx's immediate rationalization lightened inside me. "The guards were already dead. Undead."

I shivered. "It was self-defense. Those things were trying to ki—"

"Where did she get those clothes?" The woman took a step toward me. Her large skirt rattled. "Your father gave you those protective clothes. Why aren't you wearing them?"

"I wanted Cassia to be protected."

"Onyx, sweetie." His mother used a squeaky voice as if she was talking to a baby. She pinched his cheek and pulled him toward her.

He stumbled and his arm slipped off my shoulders. He let himself be tugged away.

Frowning, I watched the exchange. She treated him like a child, when clearly he wasn't. But she also wouldn't hurt him, which meant she wouldn't hurt me, right?

She released his cheek and beamed at him. "I can't believe how much you've grown."

"I thought you were dead."

He must be in shock. I fisted my hands picturing the twelve-year-old boy believing he'd lost his mother. How could a loving mother abandon her child in this harsh environment? I understood sometimes there were extenuating circumstances. If she needed to leave, she should've taken him with her.

She stroked Onyx's hair. "Your father couldn't know I was alive. He might've figured things out."

Figured out she was alive and forced her to come back to the man? She must not have loved Onyx's father as he believed.

"Figured out what?" His confusion made me want to comfort him.

I didn't dare with his mother so close.

Her fingers stopped moving and she narrowed her gaze at me. "We'll discuss it later in private."

The woman was up to something. Something evil. It wasn't just her dislike of me. It was her control of the killer Red Undeads and the fact she'd kept her existence secret and abandoned her child.

"We could've discussed it over the last five years." Pain ripped through Onyx's inflection. "You left me behind."

The picture of the sad boy flashed in my mind again and protectiveness surged. I wanted to rush forward and put myself between him and his mother. She might not harm him physically, but emotionally she'd already abused him.

"I said goodbye." Her tone hardened, completely unsympathetic.

"I thought you died. *Father told me you'd died.*" Onyx gritted his teeth and his expression went dark and stormy.

My heart ached for him. He'd idolized her and believed she was dead all these years.

The woman's thin lips lifted at the ends with satisfaction. "Then my plan worked."

"You left me to grow up with *him*." Onyx rubbed his crooked nose with a jerky motion.

The action was a clue and a tell. His father hadn't been a good one. The agony he'd suffered filtered through me and I fisted my hands, wishing I could have defended him from the old Dark Angel.

His mother tsked. "You needed to learn how to become the next Dark Angel. *I* needed you to become the next Dark Angel." She wrapped her arms around him and held him close, suffocating him. "Now that the old Dark Angel has gone, off with the only woman he ever loved, it's my turn to take control."

This woman had an ulterior motive. A long game plan that paid off when Onyx inherited his father's title and power. But how did that benefit her when Onyx inherited? My brow furrowed thinking about her response. She seemed bitter about the old Dark Angel loving Mistress Lita.

Onyx leaned out of his mother's hug and studied her with his mouth agape. "What?"

She yanked him in close again. "*Our* turn to take control."

Internally, I shrieked. She wanted to rule with Onyx. He didn't need her help. He'd taken care of himself for years. She'd hurt him. He just needed to solve the problem of his waning powers. Which might happen if I leave.

But she controlled the Red Undead. How was it possible when she was a normal witch and shouldn't have powers in the Underworld?

I flicked my fingers, testing out my magic. Nothing.

"You must be hungry, sweetie." The sickly sweet tone returned. "Let's go home. Guards take care of her."

Her long, boney finger pointed at me and I froze. I'd hoped with the reunion she'd forgotten about the whole arresting me thing.

Dropping her arms from him, she took his hand and trundled toward the path leading to the castle.

He jerked away. "The castle is mine but it's not my home."

She glanced at him and glared at me believing his rebellion was my fault. Inspecting me, her beady gaze traveled up and down. "How is she here? Alive?"

I held my breath.

"How are *you* here?" He wasn't over the fake death.

I wanted to shrink into myself. This wasn't the time for him to challenge his mother. Not with Onyx's emotions so raw and hundreds of Red Undead surrounding us.

"I never left. I couldn't leave, not while your father was in charge." Her cheeks flushed red. "Now, I don't want to leave until…" Her voice trailed off and she broke out in a maniacal giggle.

I wondered if she was crazy. She couldn't leave which meant I couldn't leave either. My spirits sunk to my toes. Onyx thought he had a plan. If his mother had done everything she could to escape and couldn't, then how would I?

"Answer my question, Onyx." She spoke to him but stared at me. "How did she come to be here? Alive?"

He regarded me. I understood that he had to tell his mother something. I hoped he didn't give away all my secrets. "I'm not sure. Cassia came down with Mistress Lita."

Onyx's mother's cheeks grew redder. Her eyes bulged from her head. She clenched her fists and stomped her foot. "You're a witch and a friend of that woman."

I shook my head not wanting her hatred for the mistress to be placed on me. "Mistress Lita is no friend of mine."

"You are a witch." At my nod, the woman's expression smoothed and her lips lifted in a scheming smile. Apparently, she wasn't worried about me. "Come along, Onyx baby."

She dismissed me so easily, just like my family. She also didn't think a simple witch could harm her and whatever plan she had concocted.

Standing up straighter, I wanted to prove I was of consequence. To speak up for myself and my rights. But what could I say?

The woman took hold of Onyx's arm again. "Guards, escort the witch to the castle."

At least she hadn't used the word arrest this time.

Onyx glanced back with a panicked expression. "Tell them not to hurt her. Not a scratch."

Even with his defense, I still felt abandoned.

"They won't hurt her. Not until I tell them to." Her evil contentment made me squirm.

The guards clattered to attention. They surrounded me.

My muscles pinched with tension. My skin shriveled expecting one of their claws to pierce my skin.

Thin as playing cards, they were horrible looking. Bones for arms and legs, a flat red body, skulls for heads, and red liquid flowing through and around them. How did their internal organs fit? Did they even have internal organs? They certainly didn't have a heart.

Or a mind.

Because they didn't think for themselves. She controlled them.

I scampered behind Onyx and his mother, trying to stay close so he could protect me if one of these things went rogue. I couldn't run because the guards would stop me. I kept my arms tucked in, afraid I might come in accidental contact with one of their claws and get poisoned like Cerb.

Cerb? I reached out with my mind.

No answer.

My stomach flipped with worry. Had he run away when the Red Undead army arrived? Had he listened to my command or was he nearby in invisible form?

"What are those things?" Onyx asked his mother. "How do you control them?"

I leaned forward wanting to hear the answers.

Her harsh giggle reminded me of my sister. Cruel and uncaring. "They're my red guards."

"But *what* are they?" He pushed for a real answer.

She didn't say anything for several seconds as if deciding whether to trust him. Or maybe it was me she didn't trust.

"They're undead and they listen to all my commands. Even to kill." Her gleefulness at the end of her statement sliced through me. A threat.

We trudged uphill getting closer to the monstrosity of a castle. When I'd flown with the vampire Moth, the castle had seemed magical. From below, as a possible prisoner, it was foreboding and sinister. The rock walls appeared to have been hewn from the cliff with a large cleaver. The imposing outer gate had been fitted with wooden spikes that could come crashing down at any second. Red Undead guards patrolled the perimeter. No wonder Onyx didn't want to live here.

He had come to investigate the other day. He must've seen the lights and the guards outside. Obviously, he didn't see his mother.

The Red Undead opened the outer gate and Onyx and his mother stepped through into a wide courtyard. I followed with my personal, deadly escort.

There were more Red Undead stationed at each door and window. The place was a fortress.

"Have you been hiding in the castle all these years?" Onyx sounded incredulous as he took in the grand foyer. How much had it changed since he'd last been inside?

The black and white marble floor shined and the red walls oozed with ghoulish menace. A chandelier of bones hung from the ceiling.

I also heard anger in his question. My protective instincts rose, but the emotional damage had already been done. His mother pretended to be dead to get away from his father and she'd left Onyx behind to fend for himself.

"Not while your father lived here." She let go of his arm and strutted through the foyer to what could be described as a throne room. "I stayed close by though."

And yet she never told Onyx she was alive. He'd mourned her.

The massive throne room had the same black and white checked pattern on the floor. Above the mirrored walls hung human skulls. I shivered. Did she kill them and hang their heads as trophies? Didn't the entire body need to go down the River Styx?

One gaudy red chair with a heart-shaped back sat on a small stage. The chair glittered with gold and diamonds. Intricate red spades had been carved into the wood. A red velvet curtain hung behind the low stage and a red carpet went from beneath the chair, rolled down the first step, and created an aisle in the middle of the floor.

It was decorated in a similar but a more elaborate style compared to Onyx's house. In this room, the pall of the dead seared my nose.

"So you were close by," Onyx continued the conversation with a strained timbre. He controlled his pain. His dark expression and bunched brows expressed the anger clearly. "You could've lived at our house."

"Your father would've discovered I wasn't dead."

So many questions whirled through my head. How does one trick the Dark Angel when it comes to death?

"You left me to fend for myself." Onyx's terse opinion had my heart aching.

"For your own good." She believed what she'd done was right. "I couldn't stay with your father anymore and in order to inherit his title and power you needed to stay. It was best for both of us."

Onyx strolled to a sideboard with decanters and filled plates. He picked up a bottle with a light brown liquid, took off the top, sniffed, and slammed the bottle back down. He picked up a plate, took a bite of a pastry, and banged the plate with the half-eaten piece down. With each item he peered at, his body got stiffer with rage. "You've already redecorated in the short time Father's been gone."

He didn't care about redecorating. He cared about the fact she was alive, close by, and clearly had been putting things in motion for a while.

I wished I could move around, move closer to him. The Red Undead stood silently beside me, surrounding me. The push and pull had my body swaying.

"Your father had awful taste." She screwed up her face.

My mouth dropped open. By the current decor, she had awful taste too.

I shifted my feet, standing awkwardly while they both ignored me. While I was tired of being ignored and dismissed, this time it would be better not to be noticed during their reacquaintance.

He picked up a teacup and gripped the item. His knuckles went white.

Clasping my hands in front of me, I controlled the urge to reach out. He might not want his mother to notice his anger and I didn't want to point it out.

She stepped up to the throne chair and ensconced herself, comfortable and at home. If this had been the old Dark Angel's chair, shouldn't Onyx be sitting on it? She snapped her fingers and flames flew from her fingertips. A tall glass popped into her hand.

I jerked back. More magic, and it seemed to be dark magic. How did she get powers down here? Did the castle itself have powers? Covering my right hand with the opposite arm, I snapped my fingers. Nothing happened again. I still didn't have access to witch magic.

Clenching my fingers together, I dropped them to my side. Frustration clashed with fear. I had no way to protect myself.

"I thought when I came back to the castle, you'd be ensconced on the throne." She sipped her drink without offering us one.

"You returned four days ago. Why didn't you contact me then? Why didn't you come and get me?" The teacup crushed in his hand. The jagged glass cut his skin but he didn't seem to notice.

Magic or pure rage?

When I'd first met him, breaking something out of anger wouldn't have surprised me. He was different now. He'd changed.

Because of me?

A light lit inside me. He'd changed the clothes he offered me. He was nicer and protective. He made me tea and made me laugh.

"Why?" He shouted and dropped the glass pieces onto the floor. "Why didn't you come get me once you knew Father believed you were dead? Where were you hiding? You could've hidden me too."

I hurt for him. I wanted to support him but didn't think I'd be allowed to change position. And in his current state, would he want me near? I was an intruder in a private family conversation. But I couldn't leave.

"If your father discovered the truth, he would've kept me prisoner in this castle just as I was a prisoner on the banks of the River Styx."

Onyx glanced at me for a second before looking away. Was that guilt on his expression?

I let out a slow breath. She'd been a kidnapped witch, who'd gotten pregnant and been forced to stay. She hadn't wanted to be here, just as I didn't. I could understand her fury. Not her treatment of her son.

"Your father didn't love me, yet he wouldn't let me go." Bitterness spewed from between red lips.

My gaze darted to Onyx's face. Originally, he'd planned to force me to stay. Then, he'd gotten to know me and wanted to help me leave. Doubts penetrated my belief in Onyx. He only wanted to help me leave because he believed I was the one draining his power and stealing Cerb.

Maybe I was.

Where was Cerb? I reached out to him again with my mind and didn't find him. My nerves for him settled. He'd gone home and at least he'd be safe.

"Go where?" Onyx picked up another plate with food and tossed it against the wall.

I jumped and rolled my shoulders trying to be small, trying not to move too much. I didn't want the Red Undead unleashing their poisoned talons on me. Or Onyx and his mother.

"Now you're acting like your father." Her voice dripped with disappointment.

I wondered how the old Dark Angel treated both of them when they'd been together as a family. It didn't appear to be a normal family. Whose family was normal? Mine certainly wasn't.

Onyx rubbed his crooked nose. A little blood from his hand smeared on his face. "What did you expect when you left me with him?"

"I left you with him so you would inherit his power and his position." Clearly the most important thing to her because she'd said it twice. "Now, we will rule."

Onyx ground the broken glass pieces under his booted foot and prowled toward the throne chair. "*I* have inherited his power. *I* am the Dark Angel."

Swinging her leg as she sat on his chair, she gave a superior smirk. "Of course you are, darling."

Her all-knowing, superior tone grated on my nerves. She didn't believe that. She wanted control.

"What about her?" She pointed a red fingernail at me.

She must've heard my reaction to the broken plate. So much for staying quiet in the background.

Onyx nudged the Red Undead out of the way. He took my hand and led me to his mother. "Cassia will be my Red Queen."

Pain stabbed my chest as if he'd pierced me with his knife. Why would he announce I'd be his queen? He'd promised to help me escape, not force me to stay. Look what happened to his mother when she'd been forced to stay. "No. I told you I don't want to be your Red Queen."

His mother gave me a half smile causing me to shiver. "Glad we agree on something, little witch."

"It doesn't matter what Cassia wants." He gripped my hand in an iron fist. "I'm the Dark Angel. It only matters what I want."

His iron fist surrounded and tormented my heart. He'd lied with his promises of helping me leave. He'd persuaded with his charm and his kisses. He'd betrayed me with this final killing blow to my desires.

Fury steamed inside like the heat from this wretched Underworld. He wanted to keep me captive.

"I'm the Red Queen." His mother stood and stomped her foot. She wrapped her hand around the orb hanging from her necklace. "This little...witch will not steal the crown from me."

The atmosphere changed. Every single Red Undead came to attention. Several dozen more clattered into the room, surrounding every open space.

My pulse pounded and I couldn't breathe. I froze, not sure who I should be running from. The woman in front of me, the Red Undead, or...Onyx.

"I can help you with your waning powers. The little witch can't." His mother's promise was a slap on my face. "You and I will rule together, Onyx." She stepped down from the throne and slammed her arm between our connected ones. "Not her."

My hand broke free from his grip. His dark complexion paled.

Gulping air, I had to wonder what that meant for me.

She lifted her arm and swirled her fingers. "Guards, off with her head!"

CHAPTER NINETEEN

I swallowed and grabbed my throat. "My head?"

The Red Undead clattered toward me with their claws out.

Sucking in between my lips, my gaze darted around searching for escape. These things were going to chop off my head and poison me. Which would be worse? Terror thundered through me imagining the torment.

The Red Undead were under Onyx's mother's control. Somehow, she had magic. Before, all I'd had to worry about was my cruel sister. This woman was so much worse. Even though I was mad at Onyx, my eyes beseeched him to do something. If he cared for me, he'd help.

His mother grinned insanely and I wondered if the years down here in the dark had made her crazy. She enjoyed a blood bath. She looked forward to me losing my head. And my life.

"No!" Onyx stepped in front of me.

My terror froze and hope flickered. Surely the Red Queen would listen to her own son's request. She adored him, even though she'd left him.

The entire scenario made me think of an unfavorable girlfriend being introduced to the family. This woman didn't just dislike me though, she wanted to kill me. I had to explain. "I don't want to be the Red Queen. You can be the Red Queen."

"Disgusting." Onyx curled his nose. "Mother, you can't be my queen."

My stomach roiled. I wasn't thinking about it as a couples thing.

"Don't be stupid, boy." Her voice chopped. "We will rule together as mother and son."

Who would have the real power? Or should I say control? Onyx had dark magic and the responsibility of being the Dark Angel. Yet his powers were waning. His mother commanded the Red Undead and would wield the authority. She dominated everything around her. Would she dominate Onyx too?

"Guards," she said one word and the Red Undead surrounded me.

Sucking in a breath, all I saw was red. Red anger and a wall of Red Undead.

Two of the guards reached out their spindly arms and were about to grab me.

Everything inside me shriveled and I tried to make myself smaller, wishing I could become small again. They could kill me with one scratch.

"Mother." Onyx's placating tone rubbed me wrong. Placating a dictator was always a bad decision. "Fine with me if you want to be Red Queen."

Yes, she would dominate her son. Disappointment dripped inside me. He'd given up so easily. He clearly wasn't the guy I believed him to be, wasn't the guy I started falling for.

"You left me with Father. The least you can do is let me have her." He shouldered his way through the guards and patted my head causing me to stiffen. "She's like Cerb. Someone for me to play with."

Any doubts I had about leaving him fled. Mentally, I put my foot down. I would escape. I would not be his Red Queen, girlfriend, or plaything.

I'd trusted him to help me go home. His betrayal crushed my already hurting heart similar to how he'd stomped on the pieces of the cup earlier. I took a deep breath, refusing to become the meek witch both Onyx and his mother believed me to be. That my sister Jinx and my family believed me to be. I took another breath, while the steam of my anger built. I refused to give up.

His mother's gaze slid between me and Onyx. She tried to discern his true intent. Snickering, she knew she'd won. "What about your promise to make her Red Queen?"

"I just told her that so she'd want to stay. Most girls want to be a queen." He left my side and slinked to his mother. Taking her hand, he kissed her knuckles. "I'd rather have you be the Red Queen and help me rule."

His words stabbed and punctured what still existed of my heart. How could he betray me so completely? His mother didn't want to help him. She wanted to rule. Why couldn't he see that?

I opened my mouth to warn him she was conniving and calculating but snapped it shut. What did it matter if he sacrificed himself and his power? He'd already sacrificed me. The thoughts tattooed in my brain. My head pounded—a tea kettle about to burst. Anger at him. At his mother. At my current predicament.

Her gaze narrowed on me as if she knew I planned to speak out against her, and that if I did my head would definitely be cut off whether Onyx wanted to keep me as a pet or not.

"You can lock Cassia up." His relaxed tone indicated he didn't really care about me. "Comparable to putting Cerb on a leash."

I clenched and unclenched my hands, wanting to punch him. His insult slashed across my soul. If he thought of me in this way, I had no responsibility to warn him about his mother. I couldn't believe I'd let my guard down and fallen for him when he wanted to keep me imprisoned. My lips smashed together in a deep, hard frown.

"Executions are so much more fun." Her disgruntlement scraped as though she was missing out on a party. "I guess for now, you can keep her."

Her statement did not bolster my confidence. My ribs squeezed, constricting the air to my lungs. She wanted me dead. Onyx wanted me as a toy—a toy he might become bored with some day. A toy with no free will.

Fisting my hands, frustration and anger pumped through my veins. Falling for Onyx and believing he was my hero, I'd been a fool. No longer. I'd never believe a word he said to me again. My determination hardened in my center. I might be powerless, but I'd escape.

"Lock her up in the cell of bones." Onyx's mother rubbed the necklace and the guards lumbered into action.

Was the necklace the secret to her control? I wanted to tell Onyx but he'd betrayed me. I'd thought we had a connection. How wrong I'd been.

The Red Undead surrounded me.

Claustrophobia, which I'd never experienced before, set in. Heat swamped my body and perspiration broke out on my lower back.

"Wait." Onyx held up his hand.

He was going to save me.

"I need to give Cassia the Kiss of Afterlife before you imprison her." He paced toward me and grabbed my hand, pulling me up against his torso. "So she can breathe."

Not saving me. Not a kiss goodbye. Only a kiss to keep his plaything alive.

I clamped my mouth shut. I didn't want his kisses, real or otherwise. But my body betrayed me with a sudden warmth and tingling of my lips.

Huge guffaws of laughter came from his mother, the Red Queen. "The Kiss of Afterlife is a fairytale." She bent and slapped her thigh. Her bones clanged underneath the large skirt. "It's something your father made up when you saw us kissing once."

Onyx stiffened against me. He'd believed the Kiss of Afterlife was real.

We'd both been fooled, but the fake kisses had made us fall for each other. My chest thumped and wheezed. Or at least I'd fallen for him.

I stood straighter. Not anymore. I didn't care about Onyx. Not one little bit.

Shuddering, I wrapped my hands around the bars of my cell—or should I say bones.

Hundreds of bones crisscrossed in a haphazard pattern creating the wall of imprisonment.

But nothing felt more imprisoned than my heart.

Onyx had betrayed me to please his mother. He'd agreed to everything she'd wanted, except about killing me. Which I should be thankful for, and yet I wasn't. I wouldn't waste my life here. Was it even my life anymore? More like my waking death.

I was a terrible judge of character.

Onyx hadn't fallen for me. He'd only wanted company and once he believed I was draining his powers, he wanted me gone. Although now he wanted me to stay. My head spun.

My family didn't love me. My friends hadn't come to save me. If Destiny had been stuck with me, they'd have already come to my rescue. But it was just me, and nobody cared. My body sagged.

I couldn't rely on Onyx, my family, or my friends. My spine snapped straight. I had to rely on myself.

Using my booted foot, I kicked at the bones holding me in. I banged on the bone bars with my fists. "Let me out!"

The Red Undead posted nearby ignored me. They stared straight ahead. At least they weren't shrieking. That would be pure torture.

The dark passage was a tunnel of some sort. The other cells lining the wall were empty. I was the Red Queen's one prisoner. A cold shiver wracked my body. Because she'd probably beheaded the rest or turned them into Red Undead. Where else could they have come from if not from those dying every day?

I sank onto the dirt ground. Being locked away seemed to be the sad story of my life. By the government and the banshees, by my family, and now by Onyx and his mother. I'd fallen for the wrong guy. I only hoped that if I ever got out of this Lukas wouldn't be furious with me.

No, not if I ever got out. I would get out and I'd get away.

The hot ground burned beneath me, changing the dirt to slightly muddy. The walls had been carved beneath the Red Queen's castle. The coppery smell of blood tinged the fetid air. Something warm and comforting rubbed against me through the bars.

"Cerb?"

He became visible outside my cell and pawed at the ground.

"How did you find me?" I dug my fingers into his fur and scratched. The last I'd seen him was outside the castle when he'd created a distraction.

Been following you. He bumped one of his heads against the bars wanting more attention.

"I'm glad you came, but I don't want you to get caught." If I ever doubted that he was my familiar, this proved it. He'd stayed by my side and was here to comfort me. And possibly to help.

I raised a single brow and trills rolled down my back. "Cerb, boy. Get the bone. Get the bone."

When we first met, he'd wanted to play fetch and was always chewing on bones.

Growling, he plodded to his feet. His three heads quirked and each mouth gripped a bone making up my prison. He yanked.

The excited trills raced against the fear of discovery. I peeked down the dark corridor. "Cerb, you should probably stay invisible."

His lanky body disappeared. The bones agitated and I heard his teeth clicking so I knew he was trying to tug them free.

"Good boy," I whisper-shouted. I finally had hope of escape. Getting on my knees, I started digging in dirt with my fingers near the base of the bone wall, directly across from where he tugged. "We can do this, boy."

A bone fell to the ground.

My pulse rocketed. Together, we could make the hole big enough for me to crawl through. I dug more frantically.

"Cerb, no!" Onyx marched down the dark corridor wearing a top hat with red ribbon, a long, black jacket with red piping, and a shirt and tie decorated in red hearts. The outfit coordinated with his mother's.

Leaning back on my heels, I stopped digging. Blinking several times, I tried to get rid of what I hoped was a mirage. He'd changed more than his clothes.

"Drop the bones." He realized Cerb was helping me, must've heard the dog's gnawing or seen the bones jiggle and move.

I raised my head and glared. Even on my knees and dirt on my hands, I refused to cower from him. *Keep pulling those bones, Cerb.*

"Cerb!" Onyx raised his voice. He didn't appreciate his dog not obeying him. "I said no."

Cerb became visible next to Onyx and hung his three furry heads.

Wiping my hands on my pants, I stood up. "Cerb doesn't listen to you anymore. He listens to me." Satisfaction oozed with each word I spoke. I wanted to inflict pain on Onyx.

"I was right." He pointed an accusing finger. "Cerb is your familiar."

"The familiar picks the witch." I gloated with a superior smirk. At least I had one thing over him. I couldn't believe I'd felt guilty about stealing his pet, especially now that he wanted me to *be* his pet.

He tucked his chin in and his frown deepened. Glancing at the Red Undead trailing him, he composed his expression. His dark eyes glinted hard. He resembled the Onyx I'd first met. The one I didn't trust. The one I would never trust again.

"Why are you here?" I kept my tone hard, refusing to show him any of my doubts.

He glanced at the trailing guards again. Maybe his mother didn't fully trust him. He stepped right up to the bars.

If only he'd realize there was more than a simple cell between us. He'd hurt me. He'd lied to me. He'd betrayed me.

"I have to give you the Kiss of Afterlife." He tilted his chin up as if he didn't care whether I could breathe or not.

"Your mother said the kiss wasn't real." I backed away from the bars on trembling legs.

His lying lips would not touch mine. I'd believed whatever we had was genuine and he'd made a mockery of it. I was over him.

"I believe ours is real." He pushed his face through the bars and pouted his mouth.

Maybe he did care for me. But not enough to set me free. Or maybe he just couldn't get enough of my kisses.

"I'm not going to be your pet or your plaything." I spat my hatred for him and took another step back. "Just like I was never going to be your Red Queen."

I hated how my voice shook because I had considered it at one of my lower points.

Cerb disappeared again and left us bickering on our own. Would he defend me against his previous master?

Onyx's gaze flared and he angled his head to scowl at the Red Undead watching us. "My mother is Red Queen," he announced loud enough that everyone heard. "And I am the most powerful Dark Angel."

I wanted to hurt him as much as he'd hurt me. "A powerful Dark Angel controlled by his *mommy*."

His cheeks flushed red. His mouth dropped open in shock or rage at my insult. He was furious with me when he should be furious with his mother.

He held his arms out and dark magic sparks and flames exploded from his palms.

Toward me.

Air scraped out of my lungs.

The flames traveled too fast for me to react.

I froze as the power wrapped around my body.

My arms were constrained to my sides. My legs bound together. I couldn't run and I couldn't fight.

I was helpless. Powerless.

My eyes burned. I refused to cry in front of him. I might not have any physical powers, but emotionally I'd stay strong.

My body slid forward. I dug my feet into the ground trying to stop the progression. It didn't work. He was too strong magically. His mother must've already helped him get stronger. He'd betrayed me for her and his dark powers.

My spirits diminished. How could I compete against such magic?

The flames continued to stream from his palms. Colors of yellow, orange, and red surged around me and pushed me forward.

I kept getting closer and closer to him. To what *he* desired.

Not what I wanted.

The front of my body pressed against the bars of bones. The edges dug into my skin, like he dug under my skin. He reached his hand inside and grabbed my chin. His fingers pierced. I refused to react. I wouldn't give him the satisfaction of struggling or exhibiting my internal and external pain.

He angled his head and pressed his mouth against mine with even pressure. I'd expected something rough and controlling. Not soft and sweet.

Who was he trying to fool?

This wasn't a loving kiss or a Kiss of Afterlife. It was a kiss where he held the power and the control. It was a forced kiss. And if a few warm prickles ignited, I squashed them down. Onyx was the enemy.

I jerked forward and bit his tongue. Hard.

"What the hades!" He staggered back and wiped blood from his mouth. Surprise and sadness flashed in his gaze. Why? He was my captor of course I hated him.

Stumbling out of his physical and magical hold, I thumbed my swollen lips. I panted, unable to breathe though he'd supposedly given me the Kiss of Afterlife. I knew the kiss did nothing.

Another lie.

He'd probably known the truth all along, just another ruse he'd used to kiss me. To make me crave his lips.

Not anymore. I'd never kiss Onyx again.

Chapter Twenty

After Onyx stormed off, I took my sister's compact out of my pocket and squeezed it tight. I'd kept it with me because it was a reminder of home, that I wanted to go home. I'd definitely been tempted to stay with Onyx a few times. Not anymore.

I snapped the compact open and examined my face, hoping I looked stronger than I felt. I was still shaking after our argument and the kiss. Still upset. My eyes shined with unshed tears. Dirt smudged my cheek and forehead. My swollen lips displayed signs of the kiss. When I opened my mouth, a speck of red showed on my teeth.

Blood.

Onyx's blood.

Maybe I'd morph into a Red Undead.

I snapped the compact shut and shoved it back in my pocket. It didn't matter how I looked. It mattered what I did. Going back to the bars, I wrapped my fingers around a bone and pulled. I had to escape. I gripped tighter and shook the bone bars. Frustration sizzled up my arms.

Cerb became visible again outside the cell. He held a bone in one of his mouths.

"You disappeared, Cerb." I reached through the bars and stroked his back.

The dog must not enjoy watching Onyx and I argue. Or maybe Cerb was afraid of Onyx's new personality. The dog had been afraid of the old Dark Angel. I wished Cerb could make me disappear into another place as well.

His magic didn't work that way and mine didn't work at all.

Through the bars, I hugged him around his first and second neck, seeking comfort. When I went to hug his third, he dropped the bone at my feet. Ignoring his offering, I wrapped my arms around his third neck. "There's no room to play fetch."

I loved his playful spirit even though I'd lost mine.

He used his nose to push the bone closer to me.

"Cerb." I bent down, picked up the bone and threaded it through the bars.

This wasn't a normal bone.

I mean, it had been a normal bone at one time. Cerb must've chewed it into the current shape. The bone was long, possibly a thigh bone. I couldn't believe I no longer shuddered at the thought of touching bones. The round socket at the top was shaped like a knob or a handle. The bone flattened and narrowed to an acute point.

A weapon. "Did you make a sword for me?"

I did. Cerb nodded.

Finally, I wasn't defenseless.

Weighing the bone in my palm, I carefully ran my finger across the edge. The flat part was sharp enough to cut. Sharper than the bone saw. Sharp enough to take down the Red Undead.

I could protect and defend myself. From the Red Undead. From the Red Queen. From Onyx.

Standing taller, I held the sword out in front of me and swished. The zing bolstered my confidence. I could do this.

If I could get out of the cell.

I whipped the sword again. It hit the bar made of bone and dinged. *Crack.*

I peered at the spot where bone hit bone. There was a fracture.

My chest galloped. The bone sword cracked the bone bar. I fisted my hand and punched the fractured spot. The bone broke in two. Cerb must've weakened the bars when he'd chewed on them. I squinted at the spot where one bone became two pieces. One of the broken pieces swayed and dropped, falling to the ground.

Excitement bloomed. I could escape.

"Cerb, concentrate on tugging the bones at the bottom there." I pointed to the spot where one bone had already fallen.

Between the sword and Cerb's strong teeth, we could make a big enough hole.

I whipped the sword at a bone on the bottom. Dropping to my knees, I punched it out. Cerb yanked with his three mouths on three different bones from the other side. At this rate we'd have a big enough hole soon.

It only took a few minutes. I couldn't believe it.

I tested the hole and could easily fit. "Can you distract the guard while I crawl out?"

Cerb disappeared.

Laying on the ground, I watched the guard. He stood at attention staring into space again. He didn't care what I did inside the cell as long as I stayed put.

I smiled. I wouldn't be staying for long.

Crashing echoed through the area. It must be Cerb. The Red Undead became alert. The creature scrambled in the direction of the noise.

Scrunching my body, I crawled out of the cell and leapt to my feet. I scurried in the opposite direction of the commotion Cerb had caused. I didn't know exactly where to go, but I knew I needed to go up to find the sky bridge. Onyx had said it was in the highest part of the castle.

My gut sank. I wouldn't let the thought of him stop me.

The tunnel twisted and meandered past empty cells. The darkness confused. I wasn't sure which way to go.

Cerb?

Right here. He was by my side.

If I could take him home, none of the witches could make fun of me for not having a familiar anymore. I'd have no guilt about leaving Onyx alone without his pet. Or should I say pets—since he considered me one. Bitterness tasted on my tongue.

Except he wasn't alone. He had his mother, the Red Queen, just like he wanted.

Pushing on, I couldn't let thoughts of Onyx slow me down. I found a set of stairs and climbed them with Cerb by my side. Each step creaked. Tension radiated from my center. If I got caught, I might never get out again.

We reached the top of the steps and the smell of death pervaded. The stink, and black and white tiles told me we were on the main floor. I scanned every direction noting corridor after corridor. *What do you think, Cerb?*

This way. He led me to the right.

He'd lived here as a puppy. He must know where he was going.

The corridor became wider. Ornate chairs with gold trim punctuated the hall. Portraits of old men with shallow skin and gray hair lined the wall.

I wanted to stop and stare. To see if any of those men resembled Onyx. But he was the first hereditary Dark Angel and I cared nothing for him.

Cerb led me into a small passageway lined with cabinets and counters stacked with glasses and plates. I tiptoed through, my entire body tense, waiting to be discovered. *You need to find a staircase, Cerb.*

We needed to go up to find the sky bridge and escape.

He didn't answer and kept going. The small passage led to a swinging door made of bones. I placed my hand on the bone door without a qualm.

I hoped I wasn't getting used to death decor. Peeking over the half door, I halted. The doorway led to the throne room where Onyx's mother sat on the highly-decorated chair.

Every muscle screeched to a halt. *Why bring me here?*

To the very room where I was humiliated and rejected.

The Red Queen sat tall and imposing. She kept her head straight and I was surprised the large crown of bones didn't make her topple over. That or the throbbing necklace circling her neck.

"Now that I know it's not Cassia draining my powers, I want to keep her." Onyx stepped out from the other side of the throne chair wearing the horrible outfit his mother must've given him.

My heart bumped. I hated the outfit, but him...

No, no, no. I couldn't think about him when he spoke as if I was his belonging.

Removing my hand from the swinging door, I fisted my fingers. My throat went dry. I wanted to punch him. I clenched my fists harder knowing I couldn't attack. I had no magic to fight.

Cerb rubbed against me. He tried to comfort, even though he was the one who brought me to this room. He was always there for me when I was in need, but I didn't need to hear Onyx degrading me again.

I took a step back, knowing I should find the stairs to the top of the castle while I still could. An urge to stay and listen anchored my feet. What else would he say about me? I must enjoy him twisting the dagger in my chest.

"She has no magic." He believed I wasn't a danger because I didn't have my witch magic. He believed he could control me.

I huffed. One thing I did have was resolve.

"As your power returns to its full strength," his mother had mentioned she knew about his waning powers, "you will be able to control the little witch." The woman considered Onyx's request as if it was her decision.

I bristled. What a terrible woman to have for a mother. I guess mine wasn't much better.

"I can control the witch now." The nickname rang in my head.

Each time he degraded me, the heart that he'd lost contracted with pain.

"With my charisma and the fake Kiss of Afterlife." With each word he dug his grave deeper.

Leaning back, I swayed from the agony. I sucked in a barbed breath. Had he known the special kiss was a lie the whole time? Was his charisma toward me an act?

"And I do feel stronger." He flicked his hand and a ball of fire rose from his palm with no effort.

His power was amazing and he didn't need to concentrate like the time he'd saved Cerb. My brow furrowed. The Red Queen knew Onyx was getting stronger. How? Had she done something to him or given him something to boost his dark magic? Something sinister? Something that might make him as mad and crazy as her?

"Good because my power will feed off your power." Her greediness clicked in my head. She clutched the necklace around her neck.

He was getting stronger because he'd aligned with her. And she was using him to become more powerful too.

"What do you mean?" He sounded confused and unsure.

Unlike the Onyx I knew. Was this an act or was he only performing when with me?

"Your father refused to consider my plan." Her lip curled and her tone filled with disgust. "He didn't want to share his power which is why I needed to pretend to die."

The woman had wanted to share power with the old Dark Angel. And now she wanted to share power with Onyx. His mother had left him to believe she'd died and now wanted to use him.

"I don't understand, Mother."

Smashing my lips closed, I wanted to shout out that I understood. Why didn't he? Was Onyx obtuse or was he acting dumb to get more information? I couldn't tell. Either way, he was in on her plans.

Hurt radiated through my chest. He was just as bad as his mother.

"I needed to harvest the dying without your father's knowledge. I needed to put my plan into action years before he died." She stood and stepped off the throne. "To build my undead army."

"Then, why do you need my power?" His voice rose with anger, but he tamped it down and glared at the ground. Was he trying not to show his true emotions or was he just a weasel? "I mean, why do you want me to share my power with you? You're powerful on your own."

She scoffed and used magic to lift her scepter. "I don't have my witch magic so I had to make do. While I waited, I figured out how to control the recently deceased and bend them to my will."

No small feat.

Onyx walked up to one of the silent Red Undead and stared at its face, studying its blank expression and vacant eyes. "Creating and controlling these creatures takes immense power and skill."

Sliding up to him, his mother stroked his dark hair sticking out from under the ridiculous top hat. "I couldn't allow some unknown warlock to become your father's heir like in the past. I needed you to inherit the title and the powers so when your father finally passed down the River Styx," her tone suggested the old Dark Angel was stubborn for not dying, "we could share the dark magic of your new position."

The woman had told him everything. Surely, he'd reject her offer. He shouldn't share his powers with anyone. She must already be siphoning some of his magic.

He didn't step away from his mother in shock or anger. He stood there and let her continue to pet his hair. "Why do you need more power?"

My jaw dropped. Wasn't it obvious? She wanted to become more powerful than Onyx. She wanted to rule this tiny underground kingdom and terrorize whoever landed in the Underworld.

"Onyx baby, together with my army of Undead and your powers, we will not only rule the Underworld, we will rule above. We will reign over the Kingdom of Alandaska."

CHAPTER TWENTY-ONE

I gasped. Guess the Red Queen's plan wasn't so obvious.

She wanted to rule the entire kingdom with Onyx by her side. An undead army could overwhelm the resources of young King Zacharye. His counselors, including Stone, would have a new threat to manage while still dealing with the old threats to the kingdom.

The bone sword slipped from my fingers and clacked onto the tile floor.

"What was that?" The Red Queen snapped her head in my direction.

Finally, my legs listened and took a step back. I bumped into Cerb and he whimpered.

"The noise came from the butler pantry. Guards!"

The Red Undead moved as one.

My pulse scudded. I was going to get caught. Ducking low, I crawled behind an iron wine rack filled with bottles.

"Stand down your guards. I'm right here." Onyx's steps came closer. "I'll investigate."

The last thing I wanted was to be found by him. My ribs constricted putting pressure on my lungs. I didn't want him seeing me frightened and crouching low in a corner. I wanted him to remember me as strong and determined. The girl who wouldn't be charmed and manipulated.

Cerb became invisible and I tucked my bone sword against the wall. My body stiffened, fear making me go numb. If he found me, I'd come out swinging.

The pantry doors swung open. Onyx stood there with a suspicious expression.

I held my breath waiting for him to leave or discover me.

The tips of the shiny new boots his mother gave him came into view.

The fact that he'd accepted the gift of clothes and shoes, that he would rather be with her than me, that he'd practically agreed to share power with her and take control of the kingdom, tasted sour in my mouth. I wanted to spit at him and yell my disgust. Instead, I scrunched lower with my strained muscles and the pounding in my veins.

The tips of his shoes revolved the other way.

I let out the breath I'd been holding.

He stopped again and veered back toward my hiding spot.

My entire body froze. I clamped my lips shut forcing myself not to make a squeak. But I couldn't stop my heart from beating like a percussion drum.

"Nothing is here," he called out in a loud, almost mocking voice. He didn't move.

How could he not see me or at least hear the clobbering of my heart? It seemed so loud to my ears. I should be relieved, right?

"You must have rats." Onyx's feet swiveled out of view. He took heavy steps and held the half doors closed behind him. He went back to his mother.

I sat perfectly still, a frozen statue, contemplating what I'd heard. By using the term rats, was he sending me a clue? I'd told him about my rat friends. No. I refused to believe in him.

Onyx's mother had been scheming for years. She'd created the Red Undead while waiting for the old Dark Angel to die. She'd known Onyx's powers were draining and had dark magic of her own.

I had to warn King Zacharye, Princess Ellery, Destiny, and Stone about the Red Queen's goal to take control of the kingdom using her army of undead. My skin exploded in worried shivers while my back stabbed with pain. Onyx was going to help his mother.

With slow and purposeful action, I straightened my legs and tiptoed from behind the rack, careful not to bang the bone sword against anything. I shook out my numb legs while keeping my heart desensitized. I couldn't think about Onyx. I hurried from the pantry in the opposite direction of the throne room. There'd be no more delays or side trips.

Cerb, show me how to get to the sky bridge. The demand was made in my internal voice.

The dog became visible and skunked to the left. *This way.*

He led me to a grand marble staircase with bones decorating the railing. I scurried up trying not to be seen. There was nowhere to hide and the steps went on forever.

Not only did I have to keep my heart desensitized, I had to keep my mind numb too. I couldn't think about Onyx helping his mother with her sinister scheme. I couldn't worry about the kingdom yet. My one thought was to get to the bridge. To escape so I could warn my friends.

My feet hit a second set of stairs more soundly and more quickly. I was tired and afraid but purposeful. The narrower staircase wasn't as exposed as the marble one yet I stayed near the wall, pausing at every landing.

After several minutes, we came to a junction. Not just any junction. A landing with two sets of stairs. Stairs with flames flickering on the edges and dark smoke blinding the view. The stairs seemed to have no support and no walls. Only darkness showed below.

Cerb stopped and his three noses sniffed in both directions. *This is new.* He twirled around in circles. *I don't know which way to go.*

My stomach twirled matching his movements. I had to make a choice.

Both sets of stairs were the same, but a more intense sulfur smell came from the one on the right. Both stairs zigzagged and didn't seem sturdy. Both climbed into the sky through flames and smoke.

Which was good, right? I wanted to go up.

There were no windows on this landing and I couldn't see the swirling lights that Onyx promised would take me home. Had that been a lie too?

Nausea climbed up my throat as indecision stomped in my head. If I trusted the wrong people, how could I trust my choice? I scrutinized both sets of stairs again and glanced at Cerb. He appeared as confused as me. I didn't know what to do. If I didn't go with my gut, I had no other way to decide. And I had to decide. Taking a deep breath, I picked the stairway to the left and took the first step.

"Cassia, wait!" Onyx flew up the last set of stairs I'd climbed. Literally, flew.

Happiness invaded like a foreign army at seeing him. His dark wings spread wide, the tips brushing the walls. He'd lost the jacket and hat, and the shirt he wore pulled at his muscular shoulders. His hair flopped with the breeze he created.

Alarm speared through my second of joy and I pivoted away. He wasn't here to help me. He was here to stop me. He must've known where I was hiding and followed.

I held out the bone sword and charged. "I'm not staying. I'm going home. You're not going to stop me."

He dodged my approach and landed on the floor, his wings folded in. "Where'd you get the cool weapon?" He wasn't afraid.

I swung again. "Cerb." I clamped my mouth shut. I shouldn't tell Onyx anything except to go to hades. Too bad we were already there.

He quirked his head and looked around, unconcerned about my attack. "Cerb's here?"

Swinging again, I pretended to go left and then went right with the sword. Gritting my teeth, I sneered, "You saw him by my cell. He's been with us since your mother took us captive." I glared. "Or at least took *me* captive."

"Good. Cerb can help you." Onyx's chipper voice didn't hint that he planned to stop me but I'd been fooled before. "I want you to go home."

"That's not what you told your mother." I kept the sword up, remembering his comments as he talked to the Red Queen.

"I knew you were hiding there. The fact I didn't tattle must count for something." He held up his hands in a peace-making gesture.

"Why didn't you snitch on me to your mother?"

"I said I wanted to keep you," his cheeks flushed, "because it was the only way to keep you alive."

I rubbed my throat remembering how his mother wanted to cut off my head.

"I figured you and Cerb wouldn't know the way." He held out his hand to me. "Come on. I've been searching. The sky bridge is this way."

He indicated the way I'd chosen. I'd been correct. But was my gut right about trusting him? Or was my heart confusing my instincts? "I'm never trusting you again." I flicked the sword to keep him back.

"Look at my mother." He waved his hand wildly. "She was forced to stay here with my father and you can see what happened to her. She faked her death and gathered an army of undead. She's bitter and vengeful." He dropped his hand and fisted it at his side. "If you stayed, willing or not, your spirit would be crushed. I don't want that happening to you."

My spirit crushed now. "How can I believe you after what you told your mother?"

"I can't let her steal any more of my powers. I have to play the game." He pleaded and he held out his hand. "Please trust me."

My mind wavered. He'd realized his mother was the real problem. I wanted to trust him. "How can I?"

Moving fast, he grabbed my arm with the sword and tilted the weapon down. "If I didn't want you to leave, I would've spoken up when you were hiding. I would've let her keep you locked up or chop off your head."

His bleak expression told me he'd pictured this very scenario. He'd be sad and furious but not at me.

My head and my heart played tug-of-war. "You said you wanted a toy. A companion." His own words whirled in my brain. I thought he'd changed since we first met.

He ran his fingers down my cheek. "I care for you, Cassia. I want what you want. I know you don't want to stay, and I don't want you to become like my mother. Does that make sense?"

It did make sense.

"It's why I want to help you get away. From me and my mother." He glanced back down the stairs. "We have to hurry. The Red Undead spy throughout the castle."

My nerves ramped up and my pulse ticked similar to a time bomb. I needed to make a decision. Did I trust him or not?

Staring into his eyes, I saw the depth of his emotion. Honesty, integrity, and a little bit of swagger. The swagger I'd hated at first but come to love.

No, not love. I cared for him and he cared for me. He wanted to help.

I decided to listen to my gut again. He saw where I hid and hadn't told his mother. He knew where the bridge was located and I needed to hurry. Cerb trusted him, so would I. To a point.

I put my free hand in his. My fingers slid into position, recognizing their place. His warm hand sparked up my arm and into my chest. "Okay."

"I'd fly and carry you up there but the fire would singe my wings."

At first, I thought he was joking. "The flames are real?"

"We are in purgatory. Let's talk while we climb." He tugged me up the stairs and I was surprised my feet didn't burn. "I don't know how much time we'll have until they discover you're missing from the cell."

With Cerb trailing us, I let Onyx lead. I'd trust him to get me to the sky bridge. I wasn't sure about anything else. I didn't understand his plans for the future.

Each step rattled more. Had the stairs been built on stilts? Or thin air? Fire and smoke billowed below as if to scare away any climbers. Or flyers. I could admit I was scared. If we fell, would we incinerate instantly or fall to our death?

"I'm sorry I forced you to kiss me in the cell." He must've taken my silence as anger. "I was furious at your tease about my mother."

His mommy. Because she treated him like a toddler.

"And I couldn't speak freely in front of her spies. I wanted to pretend to kiss you while explaining."

"Are you going to help your mother?"

He glanced behind us as he climbed. "Help her what?"

Panic skittered across my skin. He must know what I meant. "Conquer the kingdom."

He didn't say anything as we continued upward. His silence made me nervous. Doubts dug in about trusting him. Why didn't he come right out and deny?

"You heard, huh?" His quiet tone told me he wished I hadn't.

I tripped on a step. How could he help that woman? I ripped my hand away. "Yes. I heard."

He swiped for my hand and I tucked it away from him. "It's not what you think."

"Then, what is it?" I wanted to know if he planned to help his mother. My friends were involved in ruling and this information could be invaluable. I couldn't admit that to him. He and his mother would somehow use it to their advantage.

Tension threaded the fiery atmosphere between us. The fire blazed higher around us with each step we took. I barely noticed. He gave up on trying to hold my hand while I kept the sword gripped in the other. Just in case I needed the weapon.

"The only way to get my full powers back is to go along with my mother's scheme." Did he believe his powers were more important than the kingdom?

I opened my mouth to ask when we were interrupted by Cerb's bark.

The dog ran up the stairs between us and circled.

"What is it, Cerb?" I laid my hand on the dog.

Skreeetcheeetcheetch!

The shriek sheared through my head. My body went on high alert.

"The Red Undead." Onyx's voice flattened with the announcement.

Skreeetcheeetcheetch!

Dread bulleted from my brain to my feet. "They're after me."

The *click, click, click* of the Red Undeads' bones clattered in my head. The thought of their claws filling my veins with poison slowed me down.

I had to keep moving.

Onyx grabbed my hand, giving me no choice this time. He pulled me up the stairs as fast as I could follow his long legs. With my other hand I held the sword aloft, knowing that if those things got close, I could take them down. I *would* take them down.

Cerb ran ahead of us and barked.

The Red Undead kept climbing the stairs. They didn't stop. The fire didn't bother them. Their dead eyes stared straight ahead at their target.

Me.

My insides quivered. I might be wearing protective clothing but if they scraped deep enough I'd die, or maybe become one of them—a fate worse than death. No fiddle leaf could save me.

They were a dozen feet away.

"Hurry, Cassia." Onyx urged me on even though I didn't know where we were going or how long it would take to get there.

Breathless, both from climbing the stairs and the panic, I kept glancing backward.

The Red Undead gained speed. Were they magical? They weren't very fast in our last fight. I hoped they couldn't fly.

They shortened the distance. Just six feet apart.

I swung the sword with shaky hands. I cut the closest one down at its knees.

It crumpled on the stairs into pieces of bone.

Taking them out one at a time wasn't going to stop them. There were already dozens and more clattered up the stairs, one after another. An army of undead who didn't care whether they survived.

I seemed to be the only one who cared. "Onyx."

He looked behind me and his expression flashed with regret. "Mother's going to go mad."

Why did he care what his mother thought? We were leaving this purgatory.

He stuck his palm out. Dark magic exploded at the Red Undead. Several fell to the ground.

Staggering back, I watched in awe. He hadn't used such powerful magic when we'd fought outside the castle, before we discovered his mother controlled the Red Undead. Onyx had become much stronger since being in his mother's presence. And yet, he'd said he still didn't have his full power. When he did, he'd be unstoppable.

I shivered, hoping he never truly turned against me.

The Red Undead marched forward, step by step, stomping over the bones of their compatriots. They didn't care about each other. They had no emotions. No souls.

Cerb stopped to bark at them.

"No, Cerb. Keep going." I refused to give up or go down without a proper fight.

"In there." Onyx blasted several more Red Undeads.

I didn't jump at the noise.

A glowing door shined at the top of the stairs. Light seeped out around the edges and a black curlicue pattern decorated the iron door.

Cerb ran ahead and waited.

I darted for the exit and slammed my hands against it. A slight electric pulse ran up my arms. I didn't care. Time for questions later. Right now, we had to get to the bridge and escape. I pushed at the door.

It didn't budge.

My lungs screamed. I slammed my palms down again, pushing harder and harder, again and again.

Nothing happened. The door didn't shift.

The screaming in my lungs grew more acute, more panicked. The Red Undead continued to climb the stairs. They'd never give up. Onyx threw fireball after fireball. Each ball was smaller and slower than the last. He wouldn't last forever.

Cerb growled out of all three mouths.

Fisting my hands, I pounded on the door one last time. It was no good. My body wilted with loss of adrenaline. "The door won't open."

And we were cornered at the top of the stairs.

CHAPTER TWENTY-TWO

"The door opened for me earlier." Onyx tossed another fireball and it flared out before hitting its target.

A scream whistled out of my deflated lungs. He was losing his power. We were stuck between a locked door and a hot place. We were doomed. We were going to be killed by the Red Undead or recaptured only to have our heads chopped off by his mother. "Your mother must've locked it."

"You're not pushing hard enough." He gritted his teeth. Perspiration shined on his upper lip.

"I'm pushing. I'm shoving." I whacked the door with my booted foot. "I'm kicking."

"Let me see." He slipped behind me. "Fight them off."

I gripped my sword in both hands, proud that he trusted me to protect. Swinging high, I slashed the neck of the first Red Undead that approached. I bent low and took another at the knees. Adrenaline bolted through me once more. We wouldn't die here. Not if I could help it.

Cerb continued to growl.

Another one charged and I whipped the sword at its spindly fingers and arms, then went for the head. I couldn't think of them as people. Because they weren't. They were soulless skeletons reanimated to become killing machines.

Onyx touched the door and it flung open.

My mouth dropped but I didn't stand around staring. I rushed behind him through the door. Cerb followed.

Onyx slammed the door shut behind him.

Relief swept through me and I fell against him, needing his comfort. Just for a second to compose myself.

"Turn around."

I stiffened at his words as rejection sliced my midsection. He didn't want to hold me. Straightening, I pivoted on my heels and halted.

He hadn't lied.

The bridge glowed identical to the door, crackling with energy and light. The plank structure hung in the sky, a bridge to nowhere. A narrow and shaky bridge. Colored lights swirled and flashed in a twisted shape. Like a lightning tornado.

The Archeron Lights.

My mind swirled with the lights, disbelieving that my home could be so close. I peered up trying to see the ground of my world, my endangered kingdom. Sweet sadness flowed through my veins.

These were the lights I'd seen from Onyx's balcony. Up close, they appeared more violent. Fear clashed through me. My way home wouldn't be safe and simple.

Cerb ran past, jostling me.

"Whoa." I held out my arms for balance and gripped the sword tighter. "Careful, Cerb."

I didn't want to fall off. I peered down and saw blackness. At least there were no flames.

Swallowing, I peered back at Onyx.

He sagged against the door, bracing as the Red Undead pushed from the other side. His haggard face and limp body foretold he'd exhausted his dark magic.

"Are you going to be okay?" I didn't know what the next step of our adventure entailed, but I needed him at full force.

"I'm fine." He sounded stronger than he looked.

My gaze narrowed. I'd never thought of the Dark Angel as someone who got tired.

Skreeetcheeetcheetch!

Cringing, I covered my ears.

The Red Undead scratched and screamed at the door, wanting to be let in. They were from the Underworld. Could they open the door too? The Red Queen was going to be angry when she learned how many of her army were now dead.

A hysterical giggle bubbled up inside me. They *were* already dead. So what would they be called now?

"Go ahead. They won't kill me." Onyx pressed me forward.

Worry for him lurched in my stomach. "They might injure you. You've gone against your mother."

"She doesn't know I'm helping you. It will be fine." He meant because even if she did find out it wouldn't matter because he'd be safe with me. No way, would he consider staying. "Go." He wanted me to take the lead.

Blackness filled the space below. I couldn't see the River Styx or the weird trees or the hard ground. Shaking my head, I needed to concentrate on where I was going, not where I'd been. I took a step off the ledge and onto the bridge.

The bridge lit up and shook.

Skreeetcheeetcheetch!

I became dizzy and held out my arms. "Don't fall now," I muttered to myself.

Cerb barked, cheering me on.

"You need to catch the swirling bolts of lightning." Onyx's taut tone displayed his worry. He stayed leaning against the door. "The lights will take you home."

"How do you know?"

"My mother told me."

"And you believed her?" I certainly didn't.

"She's beginning to open up to me. Eventually, she'll tell me everything." He sounded so sure, but he wasn't staying.

Lightning sizzled through the sky, brighter and more frequent, protesting my presence on the bridge. The bolts whirled and crackled. Remembering the electric shock I'd gotten when I made contact with the door, I'm sure if I touched a lightning strike the pain would be ten times worse.

My insides shriveled and my knees trembled. I forced myself to take another step, judging the distance. I couldn't jump to a bolt of lightning. I'd fall and be right back where I started on the banks of the River Styx.

A bolt struck the edge of the bridge, shaking the structure.

"We need to hurry. Fly up here." If we could time it right, he could fly with me into the storm. "The next one might strike the bridge any time."

I wasn't sure of our relationship but I didn't want him staying and being corrupted by the Red Queen. I wanted time to discover what we could be together without the lies between us. I wanted him safe.

Still leaning against the door, his astonished expression changed to a frown and a shadow crossed his face. His cheeks became pinched and hard. "I can't."

His words were bullets through my chest. I didn't understand. He couldn't physically follow me because he was stuck here or did he not want to come? I thought we had a connection and the betrayal had been a charade for his mother. He cared for me, didn't he? I wanted him to become part of my real life. I opened my mouth to ask for an explanation.

Splinters cracked through the door.

Skreeetcheeetcheetch!

My pulse exploded. "Watch out!" I screamed.

The Red Undead were breaking the door down. One of their poisoned talons almost scratched him.

"Go!" He backed away from the door as a sharp claw came through where his head had just been. "If I stop fighting, these guards will get to you. They'll kill you." He seemed agonized by the thought of me dead. "You have to go without me."

Or did he just want me gone? To satisfy his mother. To regain his powers.

"Go now!" His fierceness told me this was not a request. "The Red Undead won't hurt me. You need to leave."

My heart sunk. He wanted me to leave, to go home without him. He wanted to stay.

Red Undeads sliced through the door. They pushed and shoved. The door burst open and hung on its hinges. The undead poured over the threshold. They were an endless, bloody red, stream of enemies.

Skreeetcheeetcheetch!

My body shivered from their piercing screams. Nauseous and dizzy at the same time, I rolled in my shoulders. To protect myself from the shrieks and Onyx's rejection.

Onyx didn't stop. Taking a couple of steps back, he threw magical fireballs and took out as many Red Undeads as he could.

My eyes stung. I wasn't ready to give up on him yet.

I put one foot in front of the other, arriving at the end of the bridge to nowhere. A bridge I hoped would take me somewhere.

The jagged lightning storm boomed like thunder, curling and tangling into a twisted braid and moved farther away.

I couldn't wait for the storm to come closer. Onyx used up his energy by the second. He'd be depleted soon and the Red Undead would charge. I had to find a way to escape.

Skreeetcheeetcheetch!

Ignoring the shrieks, I concentrated on the lights. They were just out of reach. If only I could jump.

Cerb rubbed against my leg.

An idea jolted. Cerb could jump to the beam. He'd carried me before. Torment ripped the idea in half and tattered it into shreds. If he jumped and couldn't go through the Archeron Barrier, he'd fall and die. I couldn't sacrifice him.

Cerb rubbed against my leg, understanding my thought process. He pushed a little harder and the compact in my pocket dug into my skin.

My earlier jolt returned. I pulled out the compact and snapped it open. Jinx had said the mirror had a lot of power in the kingdom. It might be able to reach the magic in the storm.

Regular magic.

Witch magic.

Being close to the barrier would help. Was I close enough?

"Now's not the time to be checking how you look." Onyx glanced at me for a second before throwing a tiny spark. His large glowing fireballs were getting smaller and smaller. He wouldn't last much longer.

Red Undead kept pouring up the stairs and through the door.

"You're gorgeous no matter what." He flashed a lazy, sexy smile.

My knees went weak. But I couldn't take my mind off the prize. "The compact is magical."

Or at least I hoped Jinx told the truth.

I held the open mirror and angled the glass toward the wild, twisting beams of light. "Disruption Refract!"

The light refracted and hit the mirror.

My fingers electrified and I held on. My eyes widened watching the mirror bend the swirling lights. The spell had worked. Magic had connected with the coven through the lightning.

The jagged beams of light coiled closer. They were only a foot from the end of the bridge. The other bolts swerved and veered toward me.

My spine straightened. A jump I could easily make.

And so could Onyx.

I could rescue myself and him.

Skreeetcheeetcheetch!

If the Red Undead didn't get him first.

While still holding out the mirror, I shifted toward him. Excitement held my nerves on edge. "Come with me. We'll jump before the Red Undead can get us and your mother won't be able to find us in the kingdom."

"She can get into the kingdom." His hopeless tone was the opposite of his determined expression. "But I won't let her."

"You can't risk yourself." My voice rose with desperation. I didn't want him to take the chance.

"I'm not in danger. They're not trying to hurt me. Once you leave, they'll stop fighting."

The swirling and crackling bolts of light created a wind squall. Thunder boomed as if complaining about my control of the storm.

I couldn't hold on much longer. "How can you be sure?"

He lowered his hands and stepped to the side. He stopped fighting.

Terror raced through me. He couldn't quit and die now.

He stood there wearing the clothes his mother had given him with an expression of grim reality.

The Red Undead clattered right past him. They didn't even notice him. Their soulless gazes targeted me.

Only me.

My pulse swooshed.

"Go!" Onyx shouted.

My body jerked. I didn't have a choice. My only hope was that the Red Undead wouldn't turn on him after I left. That the Red Queen would keep him safe.

With a final glance goodbye, I jumped into the tornado of lights, and saved myself.

CHAPTER TWENTY-THREE

The flashes blinded me and I closed my eyes. My body whipped and whirled. Shaken and stirred. Thunder boomed damaging my ears and the smell of scorched skin burned my nose. *My skin?* I didn't feel any pain, even though my body buzzed and bumped and lurched. My arms flailed while my pulse scampered. I was in the middle of a lightning storm.

Not a normal lightning storm.

A magical storm.

A storm that would hopefully take me home.

This was nothing like falling through a witching glass. My body spun. My head dizzied. My mind ached. It was like being in a tornado of lights.

I'd left Onyx behind to face his mother. Or had he left me?

A few of his comments speared through my head. *Eventually, she'll tell me everything. I have to get all my powers back...go along with my mother's scheme.* He'd never planned to come with me. He'd chosen his mother and his powers over me.

My body flopped and hit something hard. The lights circled away out of reach, abandoning me like Onyx. My bruised heart spasmed. He left me in darkness, lying on the ground.

Cold, hard ground.

Analyzing my body, nothing hurt. I lifted my head and surveyed the area.

Dark, although not as dark as the Underworld. The stalactites and stalagmites still stood. The rocky, uneven ground wasn't charred from my earlier descent at this very spot.

I sucked in a relieved gulp. I recognized this place. It was the same location where the battle between Destiny and Mistress Lita had taken place. The location I'd originally fallen from the coven and onto the banks of the River Styx.

My breath squealed out with excitement. I was back. Back in the coven. A coven I once called home. Laying back down, I hugged the dirty, rocky earth. It was hard to believe I'd just crossed through this hard ground.

A wet tongue licked my cheek.

I bolted upright. "Cerb."

Cerb became visible. He stood beside me, his three heads appearing concerned.

I wrapped my arms around one of his necks and held him tight. "You followed me. Are you okay?"

I'm your familiar. Of course, I followed you. His practical answer made me want to scream.

"Did you know you could cross the Archeron Barrier?" My anxiety would've lessened if I'd known he wouldn't die trying to cross through.

No. He shook his heads.

"What if you weren't able to cross? What if you died?" My voice rose with past fear. That's the reason why I decided not to have him jump with me on his back. I didn't know if he'd survive.

He quirked his heads in a question. *I made it.*

A smile burst on my face and I straightened my shoulders. Satisfaction oozed through my veins and I felt stronger than ever before. Onyx and Cerb had helped me get away, but I'd been the driving force.

Being the hero was important to the old me. Not this new version. Who saved who didn't matter. Not anymore. I'd learned during my Underworld adventure that I didn't need or want the spotlight.

Although with Cerb as my familiar there'd be no way to avoid notoriety in the coven. He'd be intimidating. And so would I. I grinned in slow motion imagining my sister's expression when she saw me with Cerb by my side.

And Onyx?

I didn't know what to think. "Should we wait for Onyx?"

Cerb shook his three heads in a slow, sad movement.

My chest hollowed, feeling empty. Onyx hadn't come, which I'd suspected. His powers were more important than me. What if he succumbed fully to the Red Queen's influence?

Anguish cascaded from my heart and dropped into my stomach. I had to stop thinking about Onyx. He'd made his choice. His mother and his powers over me.

I examined every inch of Cerb's huge body making sure he hadn't sustained any injuries from the fight against the Red Undead and crossing the Archeron Barrier. I shuddered remembering the fierceness of the Red Queen's army.

The cascade soured and twisted with worry. Now that I was gone, would the Red Undead stop fighting and go back to the Red Queen? Could she communicate with them and learn of Onyx's treachery? Would he be punished or would he find a way to return to the Red Queen's side? Would he join his mother on her quest to rule the kingdom?

Shaking my head, the questions without answers rattled around inside. I couldn't sit here on the ground. I was done waiting for others or waiting for a rescue. I was strong and determined.

I got to my feet. "Let's go home, Cerb."

Where was home? My parents had been involved in trapping me in the basement. They wouldn't welcome me back nor did I trust them. Hopefully my sister Jinx would be imprisoned by the coven.

Who ran the Inferis Coven now? Mistress Lita was gone. Destiny was next in the mistress line. Would she accept it? From my studies, I understood the warlocks should get their chance to rule. Would the witches allow it? Would they welcome me back?

The friends I'd seen before I'd fallen were Destiny and Stone. Stone had probably returned to King Zacharye's side. I didn't know where anyone else was. Not Lukas, Violet, Helartha, Pith, Gnit, or Trolgar. Sorrow shifted through me and morphed to urgency. "First, I have to warn the king about the Red Queen's scheme."

Weaving around stalagmites and stalactites, I dashed out of the cave with Cerb on my heels. With his size, he broke one of the outcroppings as he maneuvered through the cave. I couldn't worry about the damage my familiar caused, I had to talk to the coven leaders about what happened on the banks of the River Styx and what I'd learned.

The urgency flipped and scraped. Would they believe me? Would they fear Cerb? Could I even trust them?

"Cerb, go invisible until I tell you it's safe." I hoped he'd be accepted.

I hoped I would.

Emerging from the cave and bustling past the large rocks, I took a deep breath of crisp, fresh, free air. No sulfur scent. The roaring of the river greeted me. I snapped my fingers and my dirty shirt, vest, and pants became clean.

I'd missed my magic.

Frowning, I couldn't stop my thoughts returning to Onyx. My eyes stung and I blinked several times. I missed him and would probably never see him again. I wanted a different last kiss than the one he'd forced upon me. Either way, I'd never forget the taste of his lips, his earthy scent, or his sexy smile. I needed to remember that he'd chosen to stay. I firmed my lips and my attitude. I had a purpose and a goal.

"Everything will be okay, Cerb." I said it more to assure myself than him.

Quickening past the banks of this river, I trampled a well worn path. Through the boulders and rocks, the field of grass and weeds, toward Inferis Academy and the town.

Loud popping and sparks flew from the school stadium. It didn't look or sound like any game I knew. It was the middle of the day, and the students should be in class. Unless the new leaders had drastically changed things. My stomach tumbled. I should scout around the coven and gather intel before approaching anyone.

Scurrying up to the outside of the stadium, I sensed Cerb at my side. His presence gave me comfort. I inched forward, staying against the wall of the dark tunnel leading into the stadium grounds.

When I reached the end and peeked out, my jaw dropped.

A battle took place in the middle of a black and white checkered field. The field reminded me of a chess board or the Red Queen's decorating. Magical sparks shot up and out as witches threw spells at each other. They zoomed by on brooms in attack and defense formations.

This wasn't a game or a competition. They fought for real.

And leading the revolt was...me.

I staggered back. Blood charged through my veins, throbbing at my wrists and neck. My head spun.

Not me. It was my sister pretending to be me.

None of my friends had searched for me in the Underworld because they believed I was at the coven the entire time. Realization swirled in my brain. After I'd saved Jinx, she'd continued her evil plot. My friends had been fooled by my sister's trickery.

I searched for them among the crowd and spotted Lukas.

My pulse galloped. He stood on the sidelines cheering my sister on. I tilted my head. Odd. Lukas was a fighter. He wouldn't stand on the sidelines watching a battle. He'd join in.

Except he had no magic to fight.

A witch got zapped and fell to the ground in front of me.

I jerked back and my eyes widened at her unmoving form. No one checked on her. The witches continued their battle.

Chaos reigned in the coven.

I had to warn King Zacharye and save the Kingdom of Alandaska from the Red Queen's evil scheme. But first, I had to stop a witch war.

Keep reading for a Sneak Peek at Cassia's next exciting adventure...

The smoke cleared and I found myself standing several feet from my sister. She stood with her legs wide, pointing her wand at witch after witch and taking them down. A completely unconcerned and uncaring expression on *my face.*

Quick anger rose inside, igniting a furious crackle of light I'd never felt before. How dare she carelessly injure witches while pretending to be me? I'd saved her life. "Jinx!"

Her eyes went wide and she swiveled her head to look at me. She hadn't been expecting to be called by her real name. Her gaze connected with mine and deep inside my gray eyes, I saw the real her beneath the Cassia façade.

Cruel, vicious, wicked. "Little sister."

Her calm acceptance of being caught set my internal light flashing in jagged zigs and zags. She wasn't thankful I'd saved her life.

My misplaced protection of her had me clenching my fists and taking another step closer, careful of any sneak attack. "Still pretending to be me, I see."

"You should be happy I've increased your popularity and reputation." Her lips took a jaunty tilt in a superior angle I never would've made. "What are you wearing?"

Her tone suggested my style choices were terrible. I didn't care. I glanced down at the long-sleeved maroon shirt, black leather vest, and black leather pants dragging on the ground even with a belt cinched tight. Onyx had given me these clothes for protection. My heart contracted.

A witch rushed at us.

I raised my palm and without thought a strong burst of light exploded from my hand, pushing the witch backward. She stumbled to the ground and screamed. I sucked in a breath, still surprised by my strength.

"Impressive. You've learned a thing or two." Even with a compliment she demeaned me with her tone.

"I've learned a lot. Like not to trust a snake like you." I remembered her familiar was a snake and how it suited her perfectly. "Why is Lukas still here?"

Still with you? I didn't add the second question because I didn't want to sound jealous. That was the reason she took an interest in him in the first place.

The sounds of explosions and zapping quieted. A dozen witches or more were still fighting. Dozens lay on the ground in stiff forms. Where was the witch doctor and her assistants? Why wasn't anyone helping?

"Lukas, my pet werewolf." Jinx winked at me and I understood she was trying to rile me. "He's my cheerleader."

I wanted to wail. Lukas was no one's cheerleader. He was fierce and protective. I couldn't believe he was still with her unless he'd truly bonded. I couldn't say any of that out loud though. Best for her to believe I didn't care. But I did. My shoulders dipped. Werewolves mated for life.

Another witch charged at us. Jinx blasted while I sent a bolt of light. The witch fell, but not before her shocked expression proved she'd noticed there were two Cassias.

"What's going on here?" I couldn't believe coven leadership would allow this massacre. I accessed the weird magic and sent a burst of light toward another witch who'd tried to sneak up on me. I needed information before exposing Jinx as a fraud, before locking her up. "Why are you fighting other witches? What did you do?"

Jinx's smug smile irritated more because it was on my face. She blasted another witch. The witch didn't scream, just froze in place and tumbled over. "Succession at the coven is a mess."

My anger flared and the crackling light inside me, sizzling light I'd never felt until today, rose higher. "Because of Mistress Lita's plan to sacrifice my friend Destiny, and stay in power. And your complicity in it." Jinx had been helping the mistress with her evil plan and they'd failed. "Where is Destiny? Is she in charge?"

"A banshee leading the coven? No way." Revulsion filled Jinx's tone. She blasted another witch, who froze and fell. "Destiny left with hunky Stone to help King Zacharye rule the Kingdom of Alandaska."

Trying to ease up on my magic, I sent a bolt of power at another witch, who screamed. The scream reminded me of the Red Undead shrieking in the Underworld and my important mission. "I have to get a message to King Zacharye."

"Can't." Jinx moved closer to me while she took out another witch. It was almost as if we were working together. "The coven is completely locked down. No witch or warlock, and no messages in or out."

My brow furrowed, while I kept my guard up. I didn't trust her and I didn't remember the coven ever being locked down before. I threw magic at another witch and she fell screaming. I hunched my shoulders, not wanting to hurt anyone. "At this rate, there won't be any witches left in the coven."

"This..." Jinx blasted another witch.

Only five other witches were still standing.

Needing to take care of the immediate threat while being aware of Jinx's actions, I sent a zap of light at another witch and she yelped. Odd how they screamed when I hit them but not when Jinx did.

"...is to choose the next leader." Jinx flicked her wand at another witch and easily took her down. "Because a warlock didn't Descend to become the new Dark Angel." She shot me a glance. "I bet you know something about that."

Swallowing, I wasn't ready to talk about Onyx or his mother. And especially not to my untrustworthy sister. I shoved my palm out and took out another witch, who screamed.

Only two other witches were left standing. Stealthily, they approached me and...me. They glanced at each other, their expressions startled. They raised their wands in unison.

Jinx flickered her wand and took the witch out on the left. I sent a shaft of light at the one on the right.

Jinx turned to me with a brilliant smile. "This is a competition and you just helped me win."

Before I had time to process her words, she jiggled her wand in my face and the power hit with full force.

Jinx blasted me.

CINDERELLA ASSASSIN

Did you miss the first book in the series, Cinderella Assassin?

Cinderella Assassin

A Glass Slipper Adventure Book 1

She wishes she could fit in. But if humans discover her secret, her life will be no fairytale.

Ellery "Elle" Milford needs to keep her fairy heritage undercover. But after her wicked stepmother refuses to let her go to the royal ball with the fully human kids, the sixteen-year-old half-breed defiantly parties with her smoke sprite bestie... who promptly gets arrested. And the only way to rescue her is for Elle to cut a deal with her fairy godmother: All the magic necessary to infiltrate the palace in exchange for assassinating the prince.

Determined not to harm a hair on the heir's noble head, the reluctant hitwoman's mission goes sideways when she falls for the very guy she's supposed to kill. And after uncovering a plot to destroy every single supernatural creature, Elle is torn between the desires of her heart and the needs of her magical friends.

Can the headstrong half-fairy juggle a budding romance with a daring prison break before it all vanishes in a puff of smoke?

Cinderella Assassin is the first book in the charming Glass Slipper Adventure YA fantasy series. If you like spirited heroines, clever takes on classics, and unique blends of tech and wizardry, then you'll love Allie Burton's spellbinding story.

Buy Cinderella Assassin to dance into danger today!

"What a great story - super unique retelling! Characters were so dynamic and interesting. I loved it!" – Reviewer

Excerpt:

My stomach jiggled. "How will I ever get past the detectors at the palace with these magical items?"

The clutch, the dress, and my very own fairy blood would betray me.

"That's what the shoes are for." Gardenia, my fairy godmother, held out her hands and two glass-heeled shoes appeared.

The clear shoes sparkled in the light. Two-inch heels led to a slender sloping arch. A decorative green jewel topped off near the toes.

"I enjoy shoes as much as the next girl but how are high heels going to help?" I'd decided on the dress based on practicality. I couldn't run in high heels.

"These shoes are made with Elfin glass and they aren't only high heels." She pinched the gemstone and the heels lowered. The shoes became flats.

"The shoes will be acceptable at the ball, and when you go to find Arbor you can make them more comfortable."

I'd known this would be a dangerous quest. Getting past the sensors at the palace, searching for Arbor. If I got caught, I'd be arrested or worse. I might need to run, but Arbor was worth it. "Clever."

Gardenia's arched eyebrows asked what else would be expected. Wearing no make-up from what I could tell, she had a natural beauty. Rosy cheeks, pink lips, white-flawless skin smelling of flowers and cut grass. "The shoes also have deflection technology. Magic and majik."

"So, the SCUM won't detect I'm half-majik." Nodding, I let confidence seep into my skin. This deal was definitely in my favor.

"Or the magical items in your possession." She snapped her fingers and another item appeared in the palm of her hand.

A knife.

I flinched and my skin prickled.

"This is the Dagger of Justice. It weighs the guilt of the intended target." She reached up toward my head. "You will wear it as a hair ornament."

The sharp steel point glinted. The ruby-encrusted handle reminded me of blood. Blood I might make flow.

"W-what do I need a dagger for?"

"To complete your end of the *Binding Promise*." Her pupils flashed with a winning gleam, yet her expression stayed deadly serious.

The words *Binding Promise* sizzled between us having a life of its own.

My muscles tensed and the hairs at the back of my neck stuck up. This wasn't like the bet we'd made earlier today. How bad could my end of the promise be if it didn't include fairy academy? But if it wasn't bad, why would I need a dagger? I should've asked before I'd agreed, except I hadn't been thinking because of my guilt about Arbor.

My throat tightened. "What do you want me to do with the dagger?"

Gardenia's lips lifted in a slight smile. "Assassinate Prince Zacharye."

SNOW WICKED WHITE

The exciting second trilogy in
A Glass Slipper Adventure Series starts with...

Snow Wicked White

A Glass Slipper Adventure Book 4

She chooses to stay out of the fight. But when she's forced to help the enemy, her betrayal wakes a sleeping giant.

Destiny Snow is the last known banshee in the kingdom. Or she fears she is because her grandfather has disappeared. Humans and majiks alike discriminate against her because of the banshee wail of death. That's why she and her grandfather have always lived as hermits and never joined the majik resistance movement. Until royal guards knocked on her door.

Under the regent's orders, Destiny is held in an overcrowded cell with seven other criminals while she's forced to track majiks to steal their power. Except she's never been trained and has no magic. When she makes a major mistake, several important resistance leaders are captured, including her childhood crush, Stone.

Can the bad news banshee convince her cellmates that she can be trusted and help them escape the dungeon before they're all tortured to death?

Snow Wicked White is the first book in the Snow White trilogy and the fourth book in the captivating fairytale series A Glass Slipper Adventure. If you like feisty heroines, twisted fairytales, and secret identity stories, then you'll love Allie Burton's spellbinding novel.

Buy Snow Wicked White to escape with the daring rebels today!

"And that ending, oh my I need the next book!!" – Reviewer

Excerpt

"You!" The single furious word drilled into me and I tensed.

As if I'd conjured him, the giant from the cave stood in the cell doorway. And of course, his name was Stone. He resembled a muscular boulder.

Chills skittered up and down my spine. Fear or possibly the fading results of the chemical used in the cave. The giant moved fine even with the chains holding him. He should still be affected by the chemicals.

Everyone in the cell went silent.

"Look at me, you traitor!" He glared and I took a step back.

So much for making friends.

Short for a giant, he still dwarfed the three human guards holding him in chains. Fury thundered on the harsh planes and angles of his face. Messy blond hair and furious green eyes made my knees quiver. A swollen eye and a fat lip couldn't hide his rugged beauty.

My heart hammered. Just because I appreciated his handsomeness did not take away the fear.

Thank the elves the guards had him chained.

He jerked his arms out of the guard's grips and lunged. The chains rattled. "I'm going to find you and kill you."

The words *find you* echoed in my head. I'd heard him say those exact words. When? The cold inflection did something to me, stabbing like a knife at the same time piercing my deepest soul. A strong tug pulled me forward, similar to when I'd been running away and headed toward the cave. I thought it had been natural self-preservation, but maybe it had been tracking instincts.

I fought the need to go to him.

His fur-lined cloak hung on broad shoulders. The tunic he wore stretched across his chest with leather straps crisscrossing, probably holding weapons until his capture.

I took a step back.

Laughing, the guards released Stone from the chains and left the cell. The metal door clanked, locking in the majiks.

Locking in me with Stone. Without the chains, he was free to murder me.

My throat closed. I held up my hands and took another step back.

Growling, Lukas stepped in front of me. "What's going on? Who is this giant, Destiny?"

The giant's intense glare penetrated deep inside me. My lips trembled and I couldn't speak.

"You got us captured, *Destiny*." Stone squawked my name as an insult. "Several dead. The entire counsel captured."

He spoke as if these majiks were important. As if he was important.

Shivering, I lifted my gaze to face his anger. The snap of recognition I'd experienced in the cave came through with full force. Gripping the rusty frame of the bunk bed, I let the sharp metal cut into my skin. "I didn't know you would be there. That anyone would be in the cave."

"The guards said you led them there." He snarled and punched a strong fist into his other hand. "A majik. A wicked banshee."

I stiffened at his cruel tone. Any recognition or memory must be false. This giant hated me.

"What's going on?" Lukas held up his strong fists. His brown eyes gleamed yellow. "Let's discuss this."

The last thing everyone needed was a werewolf trying to protect a banshee from a giant. In such a small space every inmate would end up getting hurt.

I held up my trembling hands. "Be reasonable. We're both majiks."

The giant leaned around and got in my face. "Watch your back. I'll be waiting for you when your boyfriend's not around."

I jerked, breaking free of his captivating glare. "He's not my boyfriend."

Yeah, because that was the most important thing to say.

"Good. It will make killing you easier." He stomped his foot hard, quaking the concrete floor.

My skin went taut, and I searched for an escape or a place to hide. I was in a cell, in a dungeon prison. If I could escape, I would've found a way sooner. "Let me explain."

He pointed a strong finger. "You directed the SCUM to our secret meeting place."

He punctured holes in my chest. It was my fault. I hadn't meant for the raid to happen.

The others in the cell stopped as if they'd been frozen by the guards' special chemicals. Lukas winced. Now, everyone knew why I'd been brought here. To help the SCUM and the regent.

I wasn't a traitor. I hadn't picked a side, even though I'd wanted to go to the palace with Grandfather.

My lungs shattered. "I didn't know you'd be there."

"That *he'd* be there?" Lukas again glanced between, trying to put the two of us together. "Do you two know each other?"

"Of course not. I don't know you and I don't want to know you." The giant's voice grew louder, more frigid. "You might have skin as white as snow, but your soul is dark and evil."

And don't miss the trilogy's exciting conclusion!

ATLANTIS RIPTIDE

You might also like the Lost Daughters of Atlantis series...

Atlantis Riptide

Lost Daughters of Atlantis Book 1

When a girl runs away from the circus...

For all her sixteen years, Pearl Poseidon has been a fish out of water. A freak on display for her adoptive parents' profit. Running away from her horrible life, she craves one thing—anonymity. But when she saves a small boy from drowning, she exposes herself and her mutant abilities to Chase, a budding investigative reporter.

Now, he has questions. And so do the police.

Once Pearl discovers her secret identity, she learns she's part of a larger war between battling Atlanteans. A battle that will decide who rules the oceans. A battle raging between evil and her true family. Will she find a way to use her powers in time to save a kingdom she never knew existed?

This is the start of a young adult fantasy action-adventure novel series. "Sweet summer young adult paranormal with death-defying underwater rescues." Reviewer

Other books in the Atlantis series: Atlantis Red Tide, Atlantis Rising Tide, Atlantis Tide Breaker, Atlantis Dark Tides, Atlantis Twisting Tides, Atlantis Glacial Tides.

Excerpt

I ran away *from* the circus.

What a joke. Most teens want to run away *to* the circus, but not me. No, I could never do anything normal. Not with a name like Pearl of the Sea Poseidon.

And yes, that is my real name. It's on my birth certificate. Even though the certificate is fake.

My heart hardened with past pain. I clenched my hands around the broom handle. I continued to sweep the walkway around the fake lagoon at the Kingdom of Atlantis Miniature Golf Course. Instead of focusing on my past, I watched a teen balancing on a two-inch-wide black rail like a tightrope walker, his arms out for balance.

Trapeze artist or boneheaded boy? Only with hours and hours of training could a trick like that be pulled off.

I knew. It takes a lot of practice not to die.

Even though I didn't want to be noticed, I had to say something. "That's a twelve-foot drop into a shallow pool. You want to crack your head open?"

The guy, wearing a black hoodie, narrowed his dark eyes. He wavered on the peeling black iron rail that guarded the fake lagoon. "Who are you? The janitor?"

His group of friends laughed.

Heat flooded my face and I found it difficult to keep my head up. I remembered all the times kids had made fun of what I did or what I wore. These teens didn't realize the khaki shorts and T-shirt weren't the real me. Just a uniform—another costume.

I ignored their cruel jibes. "Get down."

My gaze searched for one of the workers dressed in mermaid costumes. Based on the designer's idea of the lost island of Atlantis, the course boasted running rivers and a huge waterfall cascading into a murky pool. A cheap plastic statue of the sea god watched over the kingdom.

Funny, how my name related.

"Ah." The hoodie guy glanced at a girl with purple streaks in her hair. "The janitor cares more about me than you do, babe." He tossed a phone in the air and caught it.

"My cell." The girl's high pitched squeal hurt my ears.

An obviously harassed mother squeezed by the little scene, pushing a stroller and dragging a small toddler behind her. The toddler scuffed his feet on the ground and smiled in my direction.

I smiled back but I didn't want to seem soft, so I changed my expression to a scowl and glared at hoodie guy. "Get down or I'll call a security guard. They'll kick all of you out of the entire Boardwalk park."

"Come on, Joe. Get down." The busty girl held out her hand to him. "We're supposed to have fun today."

Must be nice to have a fun day where you didn't have to worry about your next meal, your sleeping arrangements, or if you'd ever be discovered. If only...

The steel inside me wavered for a second. But just a second.

"Only cause you asked nicely, babe." Joe shook his dyed black bangs before jumping off the rail and onto the path. He wrapped his arm around his *babe* and then cocked his bushy eyebrows at me. "Janitor-Girl better watch her mouth. I'm not going to be bossed around by a wage slave."

The put down should've hurt, but I'd been called worse things. Telling a customer where to shove his attitude wouldn't be smart. I needed this job and didn't need any extra attention.

Or questions.

Joe tossed me a superior smirk before moving on to the next hole. Disaster diverted. I blew out a large breath and returned to sweeping the walkways.

"Mommy. Look. I'm a big boy." A bit further up, the sandy haired toddler stood on a railing of the bridge that arched over the water. Balancing like Joe.

The mother, holding a dirty diaper, turned toward her older child's voice. "Brandon, no!"

The toddler teetered, waving his arms in a lopsided-windmill fashion. His body leaned over the bridge railing toward the water. His sandaled foot slipped, and his extra-large eyes widened. He lost his balance, tumbling into a freefall. He plummeted into the pool below, landing on his back as he hit the water.

My heart plunged like the boy.

Water splashed. The mom screamed. The teens, the other families, the entire crowd in Kingdom of Atlantis went silent. People froze like they were watching an action scene in a movie. But this was no movie. No staged accident or stunt.

I dropped the broom, hopped over the railing, and peered into the dark waters of the fake lagoon. The murky water appeared about six feet deep. My mind trembled with varying scenarios. Diving in could expose my special abilities. *Not* diving in could lead to the boy's death.

No other thought required. I couldn't risk the child for my selfish reasons. I dove.

Submerging under the dirty water it should've been difficult to see, but I saw clearly in any depth. The icy water would make most people shiver, but the circus owners had loved that they didn't have to spend money heating the pools because cold water didn't bother me.

The boy, on the other hand, would become hypothermic. My talent could save him. If I hurried.

The narrow pool was for decoration and it wouldn't take long to cover every inch. My gaze scoured the water as I swam. Clumps of mud gathered at the bottom. Stains lined the walls like a disgusting bathtub. I bet the lagoon had never been cleaned. Sludge dragged my speed, but I still swam faster than the average swimmer.

Or, *not* so average.

I flicked around and spotted Brandon at the bottom. I swam deeper and grabbed hold of him, but his tiny body wouldn't budge. His stark expression broadcasted his fear and begged for help. His cherubic cheeks puffed with the water already inside. His arms and legs kicked and flayed. He understood the danger.

So did I. My body shuddered. I ran my finger down his soft cheek. *Calm down. I'm here to help.*

He stopped kicking and I pulled harder. His yellow jacket stuck to the bottom of the pool. I pushed the windbreaker aside revealing the filter cover at the bottom.

The six-by-four-inch metal cover was slimy and old, and Brandon's body stuck like glue. Suction pulled at him as the drain sucked water to be recycled in the waterfall flowing at the top of the lagoon. The strong force held the boy in place.

I reached for the zipper and pulled the tab. Jammed. The zipper was broken and the jacket was too tight to pull over his head.

The boy reached out and touched my arm. His eyes gleamed with hope. He totally trusted me.

But time ticked away. I gritted my teeth trying to smile, to show reassurance and confidence. Inside my tummy twisted and my muscles tightened. I needed to hurry.

His eyelids flickered and rolled backwards. His lids closed. He reached out again and then went limp. His skin was cold to the touch. Way too cold.

Panic prickled through my veins at the possibility of loss. My chest burned and I found it hard to breathe. Like hyperventilating, but only with water instead of air. The concern wasn't for me. I could stay underwater for indeterminate lengths of time. But the boy, if he didn't get oxygen soon he'd die.

My nerves rattled. Indecision wavered like the surface above. No one could see this deep in the dirty pool. No one had jumped in to help. No one would know. I placed my fingers in between the lines of the cover and tugged on the metal. The thick grate bent.

Another one of my weird powers that had been taken advantage of—super strength underwater.

"See the strongest girl in the world. See how long she can hold her breath. See her break diving and swimming records." The master of ceremonies hawked night after night after night. I'd never forget his exploitive voice.

Shivering at the memory, I jerked myself out of the past and into the present. No time for *day-nightmaring*.

I yanked on the metal grate again. The six screws holding the cover in place popped out and sucked into the hole temporarily breaking the suction. I yanked the toddler away, tucking him under my arm like a football. I fought against the current to a position a few feet away but stayed under the water to conceal my next move.

The kid had been under water too long. If he wasn't already dead, he'd have substantial brain injuries. I needed to take proactive action. And fast.

I settled my mouth over his and breathed into him. His lungs inflated and his heart calmed. Another trick I'd learned in my other life—performing CPR worked better in the water, at least for me.

The boy opened his mouth. He didn't choke on the water but inhaled it like air. His eyelids reopened with a new brightness. He didn't look scared anymore. He was going to be okay, like he'd just fallen in, instead of being underwater for minutes.

A loud splash sounded a few feet away. A guy with longish brown hair swam underwater toward us. His shirt and shorts dragged. Panic jolted my core. Had he witnessed my lifesaving breath?

The guy held out his strong hand. He wanted to help pull me up. With Brandon tucked under my arm, I put my hand in his. Together, we kicked to the surface.

People clapped when we broke through the water. A crowd surrounded the lagoon. I gasped for air, not because I'd been underwater but because the people and the clapping circled me, closed me in. My body flushed and grew clammy at the same time. Claustrophobia knotted my stomach. I hated applause directed at me. I'd left that life behind.

I searched the audience. Fear cascaded down my back like the waterfall behind me. No one here could discover my talents.

"You okay?" The guy wrapped an arm around the metal ladder built into the side of the lagoon. His wavy brown hair almost covered the concern in his blue eyes.

"Yeah."

"Hand him to me." His striped manager's polo shirt was covered in mud and his khaki shorts were half hidden by the dirty water.

I'd never seen him around Mermaid Beach Boardwalk before. But I'd only worked here a couple of days and it was a big place with hundreds of part-time seasonal employees.

I handed him my valuable cargo. "Where's his mother?"

"Up top. Ambulance is on the way." His blue gaze pierced me. "Sure you're okay? You were under for a while." His caring attitude threatened my anonymity.

I nodded and glanced away, avoiding his penetrating stare.

The guy climbed the ladder and laid the boy on the Astroturf grass near the fake palm trees. He rolled the toddler on his side and cleared his airway of debris. "He's breathing."

Of course he is. The guy didn't even need to take precautions. My breath was a lifesaving guarantee.

The mom rushed to her son's side.

I went up the ladder and climbed over the railing. Searching out the mother, I mouthed, "He's going to be okay." There was no doubt in my mind. I'd seen it all before.

Her eyes, bright from tears, sparkled. "Thank you."

A gaggle of girls dressed in worker mermaid costumes rushed forward toward the Astroturf where the gorgeous guy kneeled by Brandon. The show of concern on their faces appeared genuine but focused on the guy. Not the small boy.

"Are you okay?" a red-headed girl who worked the snack shack cooed.

"You're a hero," a bleached blonde mermaid gushed.

"Save me next time." A brunette shot him a flirty smile. "I'll definitely need mouth-to-mouth."

A disgusted snort shot out from between my lips. Sure, now the other workers showed up. Female workers.

Compared to the mermaids, I probably looked like a drowned Floridian rat. My clothes dripped like I'd been caught in a storm. I smelled like sewer. My long blonde hair in its once-neat ponytail shed water like a dog's tail.

And because of the rescue, my newest home might be my last.

WARRIOR'S DESTINY

Warrior's Destiny

Warrior Academy Book One

An ancient amulet.

A powerful soul demanding she obey.

A double cross that ends with a curse.

During a heist to steal an ancient amulet, sixteen-year-old Olivia unwittingly receives the soul of King Tut...and the deadly curse that comes with it.

A member of a secret society, Xander believes he is destined to inherit the soul and wield its powers. He is determined to confront the devious thief and claim what is rightfully his.

When he discovers the horrible truth behind the Society's plans, he must join forces with Olivia to find a way to end the curse before it destroys the world. Facing untold dangers, Olivia and Xander must learn to trust each other and, eventually their hearts.

As the mystery surrounding the amulet unfolds, is their love enough to save them and the world from destruction?

"If you are a fan of Rick Riordan books about a quest with love and history thrown in...this is for you!" – Hooked In A Book Review (Originally published as Soul Slam)

Other books in series: Warrior's Chaos, Warrior's Prophecy, Warrior's Curse, Warrior's Rising

Excerpt

"Olivia, hide." Gangfather Fitch took cover across the corridor behind a sign announcing the King Tut exhibition at the museum.

Swallowing a gasp, I crouched behind one of the vertical mummy cases littering the darkened hallway of the museum. The sweat between my fingers loosened the tire iron I gripped between my hand. My heart beat a frenzied drill in my chest, echoing the *clump, clump, clump* of the footsteps coming my way.

A shadow fell over me and morphed from blob to human as it passed an emergency light. The profile clearly outlined a security guard's hat.

A security guard who wasn't supposed to be here. This is not what Fitch promised for my first heist.

We go in. Grab the amulet. Get out. That was the plan.

In slow motion, Fitch raised his arms and brought them silently crashing down, signaling he wanted me to take the guard out.

I shook my head. What were the odds the guard headed for the same exhibit?

Fitch's wrinkled face grew stern. This was not a request. Get the guard now or pay for not listening later.

I hunched my shoulders, pain shrieking through me, remembering earlier payments.

The guard paced across the floor heading our way, toward the exhibition about the Egyptian boy king. I didn't care about all-important titles, didn't want to rule the world. All I cared about was surviving. Collecting the prize for Fitch so I could stay in his family and watch over the younger kids.

Fitch signaled the crashing motion again. Then he pointed a gnarled finger at me, raised his hand and made a slashing motion across his neck. My knees knocked together like chattering teeth. My perspiration *had* perspiration. If I didn't get the guard out of the way, Fitch would get me out of the way.

The guard passed. I forced my knees to still. Fitch wouldn't let this man ruin the plan. The plan he designed down to the last second. The plan to be executed by me.

Or I'd be executed. I gulped. Actually, an execution wouldn't be so bad. At least it was fast. If I didn't pull this off, my fate would be long, slow, torturous.

Like my life.

Fitch would never execute me. He got too much pleasure abusing me. Without me to kick around he'd have nothing to do. His slashing motion had been overly-dramatic. I had to believe that.

The guard strolled closer. So close, his evergreen aftershave tickled my nose.

My hands clutched and unclutched the tire iron. My stomach cramped and my gaze went fuzzy. I couldn't stand here and wait for us to be discovered. I couldn't let this security guard go into the King Tut exhibit. I couldn't delay this heist any longer.

Firming my muscles, I raised my arms and held the tire iron high. The guard walked by. His thin frame and wiry mustache reminded me of someone from my past. My way distant past. Ignoring the tingle of memory, I gathered my courage to hit the guard on the head and knock him out. Just like Fitch wanted.

I waited...waited.

At the last second, I pulled back. I couldn't hurt an innocent guy. He was just doing his job. Probably a dad. Then his kids would end up like me. Or Tina and Doug.

The guard continued forward. So what if we had to wait for him to finish his rounds before we stole the amulet. Fitch couldn't do much more to me. He already treated me like a slave. I lowered the tire iron and let out a slow breath.

The guard swiveled back around.

Startling as if someone had attached jumper cables and revved the engine, I leapt behind the security guard and shoved him toward one of the open mummy cases. My relieved breath must've given my position away. He wiggled, trying to fight. Surprise was on my side. All one hundred pounds of me shoved to get his small frame inside. I slammed the cover shut and leaned, using all my weight to keep it closed. Then, I braced the tire iron against the carvings on the case lid and the grooved tile floor.

The guard pounded on the inside like a soul begging to get out. His mumbled yells scratched at my nerves. I hoped he wasn't claustrophobic.

"So, sorry." I lifted my shoulders high trying to block out the sound and shake off the icky-ness of leaving him in an enclosed, small, dark space. I couldn't feel sorry for him. At least he was alive.

"You, stupid kid." Fitch came out from his hiding spot yelling in a whisper. His diamond-cut eyes lasered into me. His misshapen hands curled like he wanted to crush my windpipe. "You were supposed to kill him. What if he saw our faces?"

Fitch had been angry before. A lot. But I'd never seen rage fill every pore of his skin, spew from every breath, vibrate off his entire body. It was as if he had everything invested in this simple theft.

"He didn't." My voice sounded confident. Inside, I was a shivering mass of nerves. "I pushed him from behind."

"You think you're so smart." His tone was not complimentary. "What're we supposed to do with the guy now?"

The guard kept banging.

"He's going to alert another guard." Yellow spittle flew from Fitch's mouth. "We're on a tight schedule. We don't have time to deal with this."

I glanced up and down the hallway. "We could call for back-up. Have one of the older guys come and get him."

"No cell."

Right. I slapped my empty back pocket. Our technophobe client had insisted we not take cell phones on this job, afraid the phones would give our location away to authorities. I felt naked without it.

"I'll take care of the security guard while you get the amulet."

Alone? My first job?

ALSO BY

Warrior's Chaos

Warrior's Prophecy

Warrior's Curse

<u>Castle Ridge Series-Contemporary Romance</u>

The Romance Dance

The Christmas Match

The Flirtation Game

The Playboy Switch

The Billionaire's Ploy

The Heartbreak Contract

Find all of Allie's books on her website https://www.allieburton.com

About Author

Allie Burton has always been a reader and writer. She wrote her first novel at the age of twelve when she was stranded at a hospital by a snowstorm. Receiving her first romance from her grandmother, she fell in love with the genre. As an adult, she read young adult books with her own teens and was excited to find something fresh and new. Now, she writes both.

Having so many jobs as a teen and adult became great research material for the stories she writes. She has been everything from a bike police officer to a mascot escort to an advertising executive. She has lived on three continents and in four states and has studied art, fashion design, and marine biology.

Allie is a member of several writing organizations. She loves to ski, golf, and run. Currently, she lives in Colorado with her husband and two children.

www.ingramcontent.com/pod-product-compliance
Lightning Source LLC
Chambersburg PA
CBHW030748190726
48285CB00003B/748